REGULA

REGULA

William S. Kerr

Groton Jemez Publishing

Santa Fe

Regula

SECOND EDITION

Groton Jemez Publishing
Santa Fe

ISBN: 978-0-9990-709-0-1

Printed in the United States of America

Acknowledgements

I have only otherwise thanked my wife, Julie, in a pseudonymous book. I would like, here, to remedy that by expressing my deepest gratitude to her for (again) any number of things.

I am also much indebted to Jessica Shafer, who made me think this might deserve to be reissued, and to Peter Pesic and David Bolotin, both of whom provided greatly appreciated encouragement early on.

I suppose Andrea D'Amato deserves a nod, too.

For heathen heart that puts her trust
In reeking tube and iron shard —
All valiant dust that builds on dust,
And guarding calls not Thee to guard.
For frantic boast and foolish word,
Thy Mercy on Thy People, Lord!
                    —Rudyard Kipling, "Recessional"

Er...hat zunehmende Scheu, ins Dasein anderer einzugreifen, wie er es bisher für selbstverständlich hielt. Es erscheint ihm nicht nur plump und taktlos, sondern verfehlt. Es regt sich in ihm etwas wie instinktive Abneigung dagegen. Und er ist so erzogen, dass er auf solche, selbst leise Regungen achtet und nichts gegen sie unternimmt—etwa unter Berufung auf seine Pflicht. Er hört auf ein Daimonion, das warnt, und spürt inneres Gehemmtsein.

He has an increasing reluctance to intervene in the life of another, though this seemed natural to him before. Now, it seems to him not only clumsy and tactless, but misguided. There arises in him something like an instinctive aversion to it. And he is so trained that he pays attention to even such quiet impulses and does nothing against them—through an appeal to duty, for instance. He listens to a *daimon* that warns him, and he feels an inner constraint.
                    —Eugen Herrigel, *Der Zen-Weg*

CHAPTER 1

In February, the mist that filled the valley would sometimes rise so high a hiker could never climb above it. The sky itself was lost; much more the village. Going up above the houses and fields toward the trees, the boy came to a place that was all cloud save for the ground before his feet. There was no sun, just dully glowing haze. The road's direction was a guess, but there was no other to see or care if he stepped off into a clearing or the forest itself. This was a place, at last, free from observation and judgment and control. Free from identity, his own and its. He was no one and in no country.

The last landmark he knew was the steeple of a church growing from the mist to his left. He had been up this far before, in clearer times, and been amazed to find this building, deserted but well kept, so high above the village and so hidden by the folds of the hills. Who came here? No one he had ever seen.

On other days, he had looked down and seen the road that followed the river, stretching off to be lost in the west with its little towns or the east where it led to Zürich. He could barely stand to look, though, since the sun off the snow was blinding. Now, the whole expanse might just as well not exist, and he almost succeeded in believing it away.

He continued upward to where he remembered the trees started. He might try to reach the top, though he had never been there. On the other side of the valley, where his house was, he had gone as far up as he could, but that just led to a high flatness where farmers had their fields. The higher hills beyond were too far.

His coat was thin for this, as were his gloves, fuzzy, with leather palms. He did not wear the gloves, but he kept them in his pockets with his hands. His sneakers, something no one else here wore except for sports, were soaked by the snow and freezing. He did have a black ski mask in a large side-pocket, and he pulled it out, then over his head, and adjusted the eye holes.

When he reached the forest, he was less concerned with the road except for curiosity about where it finally ended. That would have to wait for a time when he could see. There was no chance of losing himself even without a path: the ways up and down were obvious from the grade, and that was enough.

A little way in, he came on a stream, ice at its surface but only for a couple centimeters. The stones on the bed were visible—the ice was almost clear and flawless as glass. He broke the surface with his foot, wetting the shoe further.

Following the stream, he found a tiny falls where the water escaped its ice for a vertical meter. The pool beneath was frozen over but deeper than the rest of the stream's channel. As he looked into it, it seemed to him that things were darker, and he remembered how late it had been when he started out.

Something strange was on the bottom of the pool. He climbed around to find a place where he could stretch out and put his face near the ice. It was not a stone, as he expected, though it was a pale, yellowish green and stood out against the black soil of the bed. It might be a leaf, washed in there before the winter started.

But it was not. It had four legs and a tail. Some kind of amphibian, dead or hibernating. Except, he realized, that it actually was moving. Years before, he had been told to watch the minute hand of a clock—one could see it move if one was patient. That had been true, and this animal was walking on the bottom at about that same speed, reaching with alternate limbs in torturously slow motion.

Caught as much by the idea as the sight, he lay there until the light was dangerously dimmed. This could not be natural, he decided. Something was wrong. This salamander, or whatever, should be motionless from the cold. As it was, it was using energy and would die.

After a moment, he looked around for a rock to break the ice more surgically than his foot would do. He reached down into the water, deeper than he had thought, and brought the animal up. He put it in a glove and stuck the glove back in a pocket. One hand in the other pocket and one hand in the other glove, he started down the slope.

CHAPTER 2

"Ich spreche überhaupt kein Englisch," he had said. *"Ich bin ein Deutscher. Raus, Zigeuner Ziege!"*

It meant nothing to the dark woman who had burst into his compartment when the train stopped. She took up her tale again, backing her request with narrative.

He interrupted, flinging his head as though to shake the words off. With a heavy stage German accent, he tried again in English: "I do not understand. Go away!"

Whether she believed him, he could not tell. Something made him think not, but she heard the conductor's warning and backed through the door. He kept his money, anyway. In Japan, he remembered, the Germans had posed as Americans and abused their hosts relentlessly.

Till Florence, he had the compartment to himself. Another woman entered there, a passenger, Italian, who took the seat opposite him and sat watching his face. He could not meet her gaze—there was no recoil when their eyes met, no softening of intensity. Looking down at his paper, he deliberated and, at the next stop, a man dropped in next to her. They talked about cell phones, as well as he could tell, and left together far to the north.

He had no company after that. He slept once the crossing was done and, when he woke, it was day. Mountains shot up, perpendicular, from the valley floor, more thickly clustered with habitation than anything he had seen before so steep. He tried to remember coming through here, thirty-six years before, and could not. Then, again, he had shut out much in those days.

So far, he felt no real identity with that early self. He had thought he would. Still, not until Zürich would he be back in old settings. This was familiar in a general way, and a nimbus of old feelings was gathering around him, but the details of known places might trigger more.

He looked at the front of the *Herald Tribune* again. The paper, at least, still survived, but he had collected other associations for it over the years. He reread Bush's threats against Iraq. What day was it? The date at the top— yesterday's date—said September 28. A year and a day since a man with a rifle opened fire on the Zug cantonal parliament. That had undermined his world as thoroughly as anything that month.

He wondered if the train would go through Zug. It was just this side of his goal but, surely, nothing would show. Nothing out the window, so far, had advertised how changed he knew things were. The country was one-fifth foreigners now, refugees. Every fifth spouse was a foreigner. Would he be more welcome today for that?

Perhaps, though he could be no more what he had been than his places allowed. If they were too far different, he would retrieve nothing. His memories of those days were abstract; they did not touch him and never would without a sensual link—a view, or a sound, or the scent of a wind.

Mere, risky faith suggested his youth was worth revivifying. He remembered his young self with bland distaste. He had not been pleasant nor taken pleasure in much. As a child among children, he had tormented and been tormented. Mixing roles, he kept neither the moral innocence of the pure victim nor the cheap dignity of the bully.

The morning darkness in the valley could as easily have been dusk. The sun was hidden from him to the south. Drowsy, he could imagine the bunched houses on the slopes as chambers of a single colossal, chimerical building, an hallucinatory fortress secured against encroaching night. He lost the vision as the light grew and the land flattened.

The Hauptbahnhof in Zürich was unrecognizable. Perhaps some tracks and platforms were the same. Who could tell? The thing was now a mall called "Shop Ville," multi-storied, with a section featuring trains. It was impressive—it would be a little city shopping district insulated against the snow and cold when winter really set in—but he did not feel the old station.

He puzzled his way up floors and out to the front where the trams had been. That was much the same, perhaps. Had it ever been this busy? And noisy? The old picture had been overlaid again and again through so much time and travel that he would never uncover the original.

He had no place to stay. Inside had been a wall of hotel advertisements and telephones. He chose one nearby, right on the Limmat-Quai. The next street over was full of nightclubs that almost surely were not there before. Again, he could not be certain. His schoolmates had spent their weekend evenings somewhere—why not here?

The hotel was not prominent. He walked past it, expecting a marquee, and had to backtrack to find its little sign. The clerk was something from an old detective film, pomaded and indifferent in a short-sleeved, salmon shirt. The little, third-floor room that filled in for a lobby was filled with cigarette smoke and American rap music.

Most disappointing was the bed. Not the expected mound of eiderdown and wool, it was one slender mattress on boards extending unevenly beyond the foot. A couple of blankets, disturbingly mottled, were folded on a chair, but the mattress itself had only something like a sheet, not quite big enough to fit. He sniffed around for odors but found none. It scarcely mattered—he did not think he could get his payment refunded.

He had meant to walk around for what was left of the day, but time zones and lack of sleep betrayed him. Getting up in darkness, he fought sleep long enough to hike back to the Bahnhof where a restaurant offered *Röschti* in every incarnation.

Back in the room, he quit fighting and slept again. A bottle splintering in the street below his window wakened him at an unknown hour. Shouting pulled him to the glass where he saw four men—Armenian sailors? Turkish orderlies?—brawling. They swung and grappled drunkenly until none could stand, then climbed each other to their feet and left, interlocked in a phalanx.

Pulling on his robe, he went down the hall to the common bathroom. The elevator arrived as he was coming back and opened for a man in a business suit with two prostitutes. They went to a room two down from his. The man blew a kiss to him as he closed the door.

Check-out was held up by another American guest, twentyish, in decaying denim, who whined and threatened the clerk over a theft from his room. He could not decide which of the two seemed less trustworthy. He kept silent. Americans embarrassed him as often as not.

Then, again, there were no people he could claim as countrymen without shame. One could not live in any country for long and admire its folk. One could like them, if one were lucky, but that was all. And he had now lived too many places—there was no scrap left of the human species he could still respect.

It was worse when one had seen a country as a child. People dropped their public dress before children, assuming the young cannot remember or judge. It was the same phenomenon that led mothers to take small boys into women's restrooms; no one minded their presence because no one granted children an internal life. Children moved through alien lands like ghosts, observing but unobserved.

He had abandoned his plan to look at Zürich first. It seemed completely new, a city he had never seen before. It would be better to take things in order, so that the later did not infect the earlier. He would take the train to the big town near his village. Should that, too, be gone, he would make a last try with the village itself.

Americans who worshipped Europe were those Mark Twain made fun of: provincials who never left their preserves till later life, suddenly confronted with difference. They knew what their responses were supposed to be, so they made those and, rewarding themselves, assumed pretensions.

He looked around the platform for some sign, something that snagged his notice. Some relic of four decades before, long ago, when the millennium was merely the fabric of fiction. It would not be anything predictable—a bench, perhaps, or the embellishment on a column. Recognizing it, he would know this was a place he had been before.

It did not happen. Either the world had flowed on too long, altering its banks entirely, or he had forgotten how it ran.

A train came in, not his. A woman to his right, an ancient, began to scold a little girl who stood close to the moving cars. The girl's mother appeared and pulled her away and was scolded in her turn. Not everything was vanished, then, at least until the last survivors died.

And he was wrong—children were not just ghosts. They drew attention and drew forth self-importance, if no more.

Another train came, his this time. He boarded and took an unremembered seat.

CHAPTER 3

After enough times, one came to sense precisely when it was proper to leave the train. The conductors, of course, had their own opinions on the matter, but these were not informed by the same practical experience as his.

Oddly, no one ever objected to the door being opened before the train stopped—these were Swiss, who objected to almost everything the boy did. That this canton was Catholic did not seem to make a difference; the people were officious as any Zürich Reformers. Once Holzli leapt to the platform, he could expect barked protests, but, by then, he would be moving toward the exit with all the speed he borrowed from the train.

Of course, it he wanted anything from the kiosk on the platform, this would not do—he would have to do things legitimately. Even the little time that took, however, could cause him to miss the 17:00 bus and he would have to wait thirty minutes for the next. Mostly, he planned ahead and bought whatever he might need during the wait in the Zürich Bahnhof.

The trick was to judge how fast one could travel relative to the ground as one exited and still stay on one's feet by running. That was one trick, at least. Another was to convince oneself to push it a bit more each time—to see how fast one really could run if necessary.

He left his seat as the Ovomaltine billboard passed his window—always vaguely annoying with its intrusive extra syllable. Still, it was his best guide for when to take his position at the doors. He grabbed his leather backpack by a shoulder strap and made for the end of the car as the train entered the tunnel that would inject them into town.

The backpack was one of few reminders he kept of his months in the village grammar school. This, and the collection of pullovers he no longer wore, and the one pair of corduroy trousers, had been his attempts at assimilation. It was not enough, of course, even with the best efforts of his friends to include him. They spoke to him in the High German the school insisted they all learn, but this very kindness isolated him—both sides had to use a foreign language.

He had picked up some Schwyzerdütsch by the time he was yanked out and started going to Zürich, but never enough to be comfortable with it. Then, he found that what little he learned was useless more than ten kilometers from the village center. Part of his memory had been given over— irrevocably—to knowing how to count in words only a few thousand people would ever know...*eis, zweu, dru, vier, feuf*...

As he stood ready to open the doors, a man came up behind him who made him think of Herr Ehrlich, the teacher in the village school. The same grey wool (that seemed ubiquitous anyway—even the army's uniforms were made of it), the same middle-aged stockiness. The same stuffiness surrounding him as though windows had closed when he entered the compartment.

The boy had only ever been this close to Herr Lehrer Ehrlich in the mornings when the class filed in and, one by one, greeted the teacher. Those moments had set the whole tone of Holzli's days, and now, for a moment, he thought he even smelled the sausages the teacher too obviously favored for breakfast. He resisted the fancy—it was too real. What was happening to Mark was bad enough. He did not want it happening to him.

But, also, he did not want the man behind him. He had seen what could happen when Herr Ehrlich came up behind one. He had never been a physical target himself. He had been the constant brunt of sly, half-understood insults from the teacher, but he suspected his foreignness gave him immunity from more. Others had been picked up—almost off the floor—by their noses or ears. The switch at the front of the room came into play often, though seldom for clear reasons. With the most delicate hint of causal regularity, Holzli could have felt tremendously better, but he could find nothing. He told himself that this was a different place with different rules, but something about the teacher could not be talked away with this formula. Something unsettling but impenetrable.

Only once had Herr Ehrlich seemed to show genuine pleasure. In March, all the boys had been herded to a part of the schoolhouse Holzli had never seen and told to strip. They were taken by sections into a long shower room and sent beneath nozzles shooting jets of icy water. Later, he was told that this was a hygienic measure imposed by the canton. It insured that the children bathed at least once a year. What bothered Holzli was not the teacher's glee at their discomfort. There was some other, stranger dimension to Herr Ehrlich's enjoyment.

Now was the time—they had left the tunnel and there was the clock tower that marked the moment when the doors should open. Would the man behind him stop him? He would have to act and see. The back of his neck tensed as he reached for the handle.

"Do not do that!" grunted the man.

Holzli stopped. He was twisting around, not knowing what he would say, when he caught himself. Why should he say anything? Why should he stop? It was habit, a pattern that had grown swiftly and relentlessly in very little time and now directed his every initial impulse.

When they first rented the blocky, concrete house in the hills above the village, his mother had been lectured for a quarter of an hour on her duties as a tenant. The walks were to be swept each day. Every afternoon at two o'clock, temperature permitting, the windows on the south side were to be opened for an hour. Flowers were to be visible in the sills.

His mother listened to none of it, nodding and *ja*-ing. The boy remembered, however, and, when he was freed by half-days at school to roam among the houses on the hillside, he saw the windows opening at two and all the flowers they revealed. Eyes looked back at him from the shadows beyond the pots and petals.

Then a letter came. It had been brought to the landlord's attention that Frau Lloyd was not opening her windows when expected nor were the windows decorated as required. Their neighbors had reported them.

He felt this topped Konrad's story about the motorcycle. Konrad Müller lived in Zumikon and, one day, in a lapse of discretion, his older brother Peter had let him ride on the back of his motorcycle. They were not going anywhere—they simply rode around the block and up and down the street. The police came almost instantly. One must not give rides on the back of one's motorcycle; everyone else in the neighborhood knew this if the Müllers did not.

Mark's favorite story did not measure up: Years too young at twelve, he had bluffed his way into a *Kino* in Zürich to see *Thunderball*. Holzli could not have endured life if Mark had succeeded in seeing the movie, but this did not happen. By chance, the headmaster's secretary from the international school, a Swiss woman, who knew perfectly well how old the students were, was in the lobby and saw him. She went to the manager and had Mark escorted out. The manager convinced her that it was not necessary to call the authorities.

The three had discussed this as they walked down the Seefeldquai after school.

"You *would* want to see that film," Konrad told Holzli with guttural confidence.

"Why do you say that?" But Holzli knew why.

"Well, given what your father does."

Holzli made a face at the German boy. Konrad would not let this rest though it had long since become tiresome beyond bearing. "Will you stop it? That was never funny."

"It is not meant to be. It is true."

Holzli could well believe that, at some level, not very far down, Konrad was serious. It would explain his persistence in this stupidity. "There actually are real cultural attachés," he said.

He had made this response before and knew it did not work.

"Oh, right!" snorted the other. Every time he talked, there was some audible passage of air. "Americans can really expect to have a lot of cultural influence."

This, or versions of it, was old too.

Secretly, Holzli hoped that Konrad was right about his father. Romanticism recommended it. Nothing about his father helped the case, however. Only he and the Swiss still wore sweater vests. A balding, mustachioed man in round spectacles who parted his hair high on the side and slicked it back with Vitalis imported in bulk on his trips back from Washington, he was working against type even by joining the Foreign Service. A Princeton Ph.D. in art history, he had left his teaching position in New Jersey three years before. They spent a year in Virginia and two in Taipei before coming to Switzerland. Never had Holzli seen the tiniest sign that the new job had an underside. Or any side more vibrant than the university post had had.

His father sympathized with the locals, even against his wife, on all questions of decorum. He was not appalled, as Holzli wanted, when he related the other boys' stories.

"You probably shouldn't spend much time with this Müller boy," was his only response.

"Just because of the motorcycle?"

"Why isn't that enough?"

The son did not, in fact, stop hanging around with Konrad to the small extent he was able. They lived too far apart to have much of a friendship, but they talked to and from the tram stop and during free times at school.

He shoved the door open.

"I said that you must not do that!" sputtered the voice from behind.

He could see the ruins of the ancient fortress on the high ground of the town, which meant they were about to hit the station. Good. The man might not be willing to grab him, but Holzli could not rely on that. Authority recognized no personal boundaries.

Whatever more the man was saying now was lost to the brakes and the echoes in the station. The platform was there before him but streaming by too fast. He could not do it. But he felt a hand on his upper arm and he jumped.

He surprised himself for about five meters and began to think he would keep his feet. Then his head outpaced his legs. All he could think to do was hold the backpack in front with both hands. When he fell, he still carried enough speed to slide five meters more, arching to keep his weight on the pack.

There were shouts to which he gave vague attention, but, mostly, he wanted to achieve the anonymity of the street outside the station and check his knees. They stung. Right now, he could not afford the time to look.

Outside, around the corner, near the ticket window for the buses, he could inspect his knees directly. His trousers no longer covered them. The knees themselves were not in too bad a shape, though bloody. His backpack and his shoes were the bad news: the platform had ripped at all his leather, peeling away the surfaces and leaving scuffed disasters.

The pack was no real problem since he did not need to use it. The kids at the international school thought it an affectation anyway. The pants and shoes would need a cover story. Fortunately, he had the bus ride still to go.

That would give him half an hour, as long again as the ride from Zürich. The bus had not yet come, though, and he felt vulnerable. Someone who had seen him in the station could discover him. He stood with the backpack shielding his knees and watched the edge of the building around which they would come. He thought of the words of the song they sang in the *Pfadfinder—"Der Teufel kam, gerade um die Ecke."* The devil came, right around the corner.

The *Pfadfinder*—the Boy Scouts—still gave him a social presence in the village. A cookout was coming up in the hills above the village. He was to bring servalats, which he thought might be napkins but were probably food.

The uniform was the one cool thing he would carry away from this whole ordeal, though he knew what the international school students would think of it. The *Pfadi* wore Mountie hats, like Baden-Powell himself, and carried daggers at their sides. He had broken the point of his, throwing it at a tree, something he regretted as much as anything in his life.

That summer, the troop had gone to Graubünden, far to the southeast, for a week. In their camp in the mountains, he had felt more isolated from every familiar thing than ever in his experience.

The place itself was strangeness beyond strangeness. He had decided the locals were speaking Romansch, the fabled Latin dialect. He was never certain, though—it could simply have been Schwyzerdütsch of an especially alien kind.

Mostly, they hiked an enormous nature preserve. This had been an eternity of frustrated hope: every seeming summit turned out to be a fold with another promised summit beyond. He grew cynical about the vistas that sent the other into raptures. When you've seen one mountain, he began to repeat to himself, you've seen them all. Every trampled flower brought rebukes and secret satisfaction.

They traded off sleeping in tents and dormitories, alternating each night. He got little sleep. They froze in the tents, and he was kept awake by a need to urinate and a reluctance to brave the further cold outside. In the dormitories, they all lay on one mattress twenty meters wide, reading Asterix with flashlights under the blankets.

Food tended to be cheese, which he could not digest. He survived on bare noodles and one dinner of sausages, which he started eating skin and all until shown otherwise. Only his stint as altar boy for the Catholic Mass let him feel grounded.

When the week was up, he had lost ten pounds, which he counted a gain. The greater gain was a sense of initiation— though, into what, he had never yet been able to say.

Rum-ba-di-bum, der Stiel ischt krumm, Teufel um die Ecke, Rum-ba-di-bum, he sang in his head. The bus came and he boarded, showing his pass. He leaned against the window, watching the town fade out, its last trickle of buildings finally giving way to fields. He had noticed that smells graded off in either direction, too. From Zürich on, the scents of exhaust pipes and smokestacks weakened until, somewhere during this ride, they were scarcely noticed. Animal odors grew in the same measure until the bus released him at the bottom of his hill. They reached their peak there among the cows and manure and mud and piss.

He did not remember worrying about such things in New Jersey. Washington had been all fumes. Taipei had combined so many aromas that any transitions were blurred out. The Asian city awakened him to odor as one of the world's faces but also overwhelmed him. Switzerland had its own richness, but it was an ordered one.

Zürich and the village were their own places. If he lived in the city like most of his classmates, he supposed he would be like them, almost unaware that Switzerland was not just a big international school. They complained about the Swiss but saw them as intruders on the proper nature of things, to be avoided and evaded. For him, the Swiss were the medium in which he lived and moved and had his being.

Most of the Americans in his class had come from Centralia, Michigan. Their fathers worked for a chemical company with some sort of interests in Europe. The children had known each other back home and continued their lives as though nothing had changed by their translation. They lived in the same neighborhoods and spent their free time in the same clubs.

This made him think again of Mark, who must have been an outcast even in Michigan. Mark's family lived in Zollikon, like many of the chemical people, but the boy himself never seemed to have been to the parties the others discussed. He was not particularly friendly with any of them during school, either. Holzli understood this: Mark was odd and, until recently, not in an interesting way.

That, at least, has changed, Holzli reflected as the bus entered his village and slowed. It would not help Mark's social life if the kids knew just how odd he had become, but he was no longer a bore.

As he stood and lifted his backpack, Holzli remembered that he still needed a story to cover the damage. As usual, he had lost focus and time. Well, there was still the climb up the hill.

CHAPTER 4

They came together by default.

For an hour each day, the students were let loose in a park on the lake shore. An area bordering the Seefeldquai was clear enough to allow a baseball diamond. An immense old elm tree anchored things—it stood behind home plate and was big enough to back up catchers and keep the ball out of the street. A lesser tree directed the baseline toward first, and a round, stone water fountain stood behind second. Third base was fixed by interpolation.

Konrad had no background in baseball and was too contemptuous to learn. He shone at soccer during regular P.E. periods, and Holzli suspected he did not want to damage the prestige he gained by that.

Holzli could not bring himself to join in. Transferring in near the end of the term, he found that one of the Centralia set had established himself as permanent pitcher, independent of which side was up. Holzli's suggestion that they alternate, representing teams, met with general outrage. He would have taken another position, but the intensity of the children's response so shook him that he did not have the heart to play.

Mark would have played had anyone been willing to use him, but this was not going to happen. Blind in one eye—the left, the one that looked out and away whatever the other was doing—he never knew where the ball was. The other students had discovered this long ago, and his sports career had ended.

While the others played, the three of them walked around the park or along the lake. Directly across from the school, a kiosk sold newspapers, magazines, cigarettes and candy—they always ended up there at last.

Holzli searched through his change for enough *Rappen* to buy a tube of Smarties. They were not quite M&M's—they tasted minty and melted in your hand—but they did for the time. Switzerland had better to offer. The most interesting were unknown in the U.S.—cordials filled with brandies or liqueurs, the big *Maikäfer,* and, most wonderful of all, truffles. Even the little squares with the polar bears on the wrapper were better than American or English chocolate, but the kiosk had a limited stock.

"I don't have any money today," Mark mentioned as casually as he could.

"That is unfortunate," said Konrad as he tilted his soft drink back.

The cap on Holzli's tube was embossed with a "T." Everyone collected these, trying to assemble the entire alphabet, though it was not clear why. "Yeah, unfortunate."

Mark had a gift for looking pathetic, but not in a way that drew sympathy. Holzli worked not to despise him when he put on this face, knowing how naturally it came to him, but it was hard. He understood the other kids' treatment of Mark and might have joined them had they been less objectionable themselves. Why everyone let the Americans set the tone and rules he could not understand.

After a minute, Mark asked them to share, as they had known he would.

"No!" Holzli protested. "Why didn't you bring your own money?"

He looked to Konrad for support, but the German held his bottle out to Mark. Holzli snorted in disgust and disappointment.

"He is more depressed than usual," Konrad offered in justification.

Words like "depressed" did not come easily to Holzli. He knew the word but could not have used it without embarrassment. His admiration for Konrad was partly rooted in Konrad's willingness to display his vocabulary.

"Oh, are you...depressed?" he asked Mark.

Mark did not answer and looked away across the lake. Distantly, amid the traffic noises from the main street nearby, a tram screeched. Mark looked in that direction, though there was nothing to be seen with all the buildings between.

All three stood there, silent. Holzli was caught by Konrad's face as that one, in turn, watched Mark's. The wind shifted, and the sound of a transistor radio was carried from the park. It would not be long before a Swiss came along to put an end to that and restore nature and traffic to their places.

"I hate that song," said Holzli to stir the moment and start things moving again.

"Everyone does," mumbled Mark.

"Well, not the chemical people. They love it. The group didn't even write the music—my father says Clementi wrote it. It's from a sonata."

He knew who Clementi was from pieces he had worked on before his parents gave up and let him quit piano. The others would not know, however, so this was worth saying.

They let it pass. "The *other* chemical people. I'm one of them—I'm from Michigan too."

"But you're not one of those." Holzli gestured.

The other American was silent again and looked down at his shoes. The wind changed and blew the music away.

"What is wrong?" Konrad asked.

Holzli saw now that Mark's eyes were filmed with tears, just on the point of breaking and flowing. He was shocked, and ashamed not to have noticed before. Still, this made Mark even harder to take. It made him moist.

Holzli thought of the slugs one met everywhere in and around the village. He hated them as much as anything he had faced in his time here. They were vile beyond endurance and could not be escaped. Just the other day he had almost stepped on one—only barely noticed it in time—ten centimeters long and orange.

He shuddered.

"Can I talk to you?" asked Mark.

This threw Holzli, and he could say nothing for a moment. Then he managed a hesitant "Sure."

Mark said nothing further but stood and stared at Konrad until they realized he had been the only one addressed.

"Just me?" asked Konrad.

"Yes...please." Mark's eyes shifted toward Holzli for a second then back again. It was an acknowledgement, despite himself, but a rejection. The "please," then, had been as much for Holzli to leave as for Konrad to listen.

"Okay, I suppose," Konrad replied with a wide-eyed, helpless glance at Holzli.

Holzli shrugged and walked slowly off, not knowing how long this would take or where to go. He turned toward the school, a converted mansion with a central dome that topped an open stairwell. Their break was not up—he did not want to go there. That left the lake, where he would be conspicuously solitary, or the park. The latter would be a longer walk, at least, though he had no interest in arriving.

Halfway there and about to cross the street, he felt himself suspended. Racket from ducks balanced the shouts of the game. He was neither here nor there, and unaffiliated. The moment clung to him—he made no progress though he walked. There was no danger of reaching the park. He would need no subsequent decisions.

Then he was too near the big elm and had to cross to it. Things started again. He could not hear the ducks. Swiveling as he walked, he saw the two boys by the kiosk. Mark's hands were moving to accompany some narrative while Konrad stood motionless.

A car was coming, and Holzli ran for the tree. Gaining the sidewalk, he slowed to a trot that carried him up to a group waiting to bat. He took a position to the side and watched.

"What do *you* want?" a girl asked. She scowled. Margaret Owens was one of the worst of the chemical people: she had been hostile from his first day—most of the others had needed a week or more to find their own occasions. His offer to pitch had then set a seal on things.

He shrugged again and would have started the walk back to the kiosk, but the distant sound of the bell announced that it was time to return.

It was not until school let out and Mark had left them to make his way south that Holzli could question Konrad.

"It was very personal," he was told, "and he did not want you to know. I said I would not tell you anything."

"But what did he say?"

"Well, it is a highly interesting story."

Konrad ran his hand through his hair—blond almost to white, mussed by a caprice of the lake breeze. "It is about the day before yesterday. You remember he did not come yesterday."

Holzli had not given it much thought, but, in fact, Mark had been missing the day before.

"You did not take the tram," continued the other. "You were going to walk to Franz Carl Weber's and then the Hauptbahnhof. Mark wanted to go also—he did not tell you—but it is too far out of his way.

"But it made him want to do something different. Usually, he walks down the Bellerivestrasse and crosses over to the Dufourstrasse. The little street his house is on, the Gstadstrasse, comes off of that, downhill. He lives near the top.

"The day before yesterday, he just kept going until the Bellerivestrasse changed its name and he turned uphill on the Gstadstrasse when he got to it."

"So that's his idea of adventure."

Konrad smiled a dutiful smile and went on. "The hill gets pretty steep, so he stopped to rest. He says there is a house there with a plaque that tells that something happened there. He stopped near there."

He himself paused as though to catch his breath. His listener held back from interruption—less from courtesy than because this unexpectedly sounded interesting.

"He was about to start the climb again when, suddenly, his head felt funny. Everything had light around it."

"Aura! He was having a migraine!" Holzli knew migraines well. He had one every Sunday evening with pitiless regularity.

"Well, maybe, I suppose. But that is not how he tells it. He says the lights got brighter and brighter until he could not see anything. Then they began to go away, and..."

He paused again.

His audience was not so patient now. The "and" had too much dramatic power. "And what?"

"And...things were different. Some were the same, like the size of the street, but other things had changed."

Holzli did not even wait for a pause this time. "Changed how?"

Konrad flinched and Holzli knew his voice had been too sharp. He hated to show excitement and he felt himself blushing. "Sorry. But, changed how?"

"This is the part that bothers him most. Some of the change was subtle. He realized later that the sun was moved and there was much dust. But most buildings were completely different. Most had disappeared, actually. And there were no parked cars—houses and walls came right up to the street—and there were animals."

"Animals?"

"Chickens and horses and cows. He really seems to have noticed them because of the smell. And straw was all around. And other things."

"What about people?"

"He did not say anything about them. It did not last very long anyway. The thing with the lights happened again and all was normal."

The blond boy stopped yet again.

"And then what?"

"What do you mean 'and then what?' That is enough."

"What does he think happened?"

"He has no idea. That is why he is so afraid."

They had halted on the street, but Holzli now thought of the train he needed to catch. It was long between the trains he could take. He motioned Konrad toward the corner that led to the tram stop.

As they walked, he asked, "Did he tell his parents?"

"No, he is too afraid. He hopes it will not happen again and he does not want them to think something is wrong with him,"

"Something is wrong with him if he's telling the truth." Holzli reflected for a moment. "It's not true, though. This is just another one of his stories, like that flying saucer. He didn't say he saw that till after he started reading all those U.F.O. books. He even lies about not having money so he doesn't have to pay for anything."

"I do not think this is a lie. He is too disturbed."

They reached the stop, but no trams were in sight.

"Why didn't he want me to hear this?"

"Because you would say the kind of things you are saying"

"Well, then, he was smart."

They heard a tram and looked up to watch it come, blue and white boxes jerking up the tracks in tandem. A purple square asserted "4."

"Okay, here's mine," said Holzli, searching for his pass.

"He may not be telling a story. I do not think he is."

"You gave him your drink, though. I've learned better."

CHAPTER 5

Early in September, three privates at Ft. Dix were court-martialed for refusing to go to Vietnam. This drew Holzli's attention mostly because it happened in New Jersey, not all too far from where he had lived.

He had seen his first protest against the war early in the year, waiting outside the building that housed the consulate and his father's office. His father was taking him to lunch. It was a full-day holiday for the village school, and he was being treated to a day in Zürich—back when that still had novelty.

It was a small group, conservatively dressed and orderly. Some of them waved to him where he sat on the steps watching them. He waved back, unsure if they knew he was American.

He knew there were protests in the U.S. but had never witnessed one. He also knew that Konrad's father, Eberhard Müller, was in Switzerland somehow in connection with antiwar activities. Whether his own father knew this, he could not tell—it might explain the man's attitude toward Konrad, however.

When his father emerged that day in February, he took no notice of the protesters, though they called to him. Whether that was a pose, Holzli could not judge. Even with eleven years' experience, he was not good at interpreting his father. Still, he was never taken to the office again. When he was transferred to the school in Zürich and began to get his bearings, he found that the consulate was in easy walking distance of the school. He was never given a ride to or from the city.

They rarely talked about politics. The boy was never moved to bring up such things. The man was sometimes given to short, aphoristic distillations of his thoughts, but he was grudging even with these. As best as Holzli could tell, a dialogue ran in his father's head his whole waking life—discourse that broke through into the public world from time to time when it became too heated to contain. His words to his son were like steam bled off to lower pressure.

Once, while they were still in Taiwan, his father had said more. Holzli did not have his new name yet; he was still Woody, and his classmates had discovered what that came from. At dinner with his parents, finally in tears, he wrestled with a tightened throat to tell how fiercely he hated his name.

"How could you do this to me? Why would anyone stick anyone with 'Woodrow Wilson'?"

His mother deferred to her spouse, who, Holzli was aware, carried the guilt for it. His father scarcely responded, lifting a bit of potato into his mouth and chewing before raising the fork again to signal that words were to come. Swallowing, he said, "Be glad it's not 'Franklin Delano'. It was a close race." He took another bite and slowly chewed while Holzli waited.

"Wilson was arguably the greater man, though. It was he who first recognized the magnitude of our international responsibilities and directed us to them. Roosevelt went further than Wilson, yes, but he could only do what he did because the way had been made plain.

"You'd feel better about your name if you knew more about your namesake. I can suggest some reading if you want. He wasn't simply visionary in his foreign policy—he understood that Washington had to become more active at home as well. Power needed to be more centralized if America was to play its role on the world stage."

Something in some deep chamber of the boy's memory resonated with this. It was not the content of what was said, but the tone or manner. A moment of perplexity and he had it: this was his father's old academic voice.

Years before, much younger, he had sometimes been set in a chair in the lecture hall during his father's classes. It was an alternative to babysitters. This was the voice his father adopted for the classroom. But more: it was the voice his father used with his colleagues and they with him, even, as now, over meals. Only now, dragging out old pictures that had lain in storage for years, did it strike Holzli how funny it really was that these people could not converse—they could only lecture each other.

Then he thought how long it was since he observed even that. He had not seen his father in a social situation in years. No one ever came to dinner. In some sense, he suspected, his father no longer had colleagues.

"You hear him criticized sometimes for his anti-Communist measures—his so-called 'Red Scare'—but until we had the Germans for an enemy there wasn't much for Americans to unite against. He realized that something was needed to pull us together into a country—a real unity instead of a collection of competing interests. The war was more effective in doing that, but it took time for us to get involved.

"We only have our present position in the world because we became the kind of nation that merits it, and Wilson started the change."

Holzli's notion of his father's politics had to be pieced together over time from scraps. That mealtime lecture had been one of the bigger pieces. The sporadic dicta could be fitted together to add some consistency. There were other clues, as well.

One item had especially impressed Holzli; it just had to be significant—it was too remarkable. It was a plaque his father had been given by the embassy staff in Taipei when he was reassigned to Zürich. Bronze, mounted on a stand of cherry wood, it had sat on his father's desk the one time Holzli visited his office, proclaiming:

'Tis thine alone, with awful sway,
To rule mankind, and make the world obey,
Disposing peace and war by thy own majestic way;
To tame the proud, the fetter'd slave to free:
These are imperial arts, and worthy thee.

Though he saw it only briefly, it became his ideal of beauty. He thought the poetry as elegant as the finished wood and as brilliant as the polished metal. The plaque united visual and aural excellence—and something else. Whomever it addressed (presumably not his father, originally) and whatever was promised were grand beyond anything he knew in this world.

If his father and his father's job could be seen this way, with their nobility, invisible until that moment, uncovered by this incantation, then there was more and better to the world than he could easily believe. Further: beauty and goodness somehow had a part even in the least of things. And, if that was true, then maybe they had a part in the worst.

Or, it occurred to him later, beauty was not to be trusted.

"It's from Vergil," his father said when asked. "The Dryden translation, which almost has the authority of the Latin. I'll lend it to you if you want."

The boy then understood why people spoke of hearts leaping. When his mistake was clear to him—the book was offered, not the plaque (thank God he had not shown his hopes)—he felt as if he had been punched in the stomach. He did borrow the book, but did not get far in it. He was never asked to return it, and it still lay on his bookcase.

His name remained unbeautiful—words were not magic in his father's mouth. The move to Switzerland looked like a reprieve. The name would just be foreign to the Swiss, not comical. That was true for the Chinese, too, but in Taiwan he spent most of his time with Americans. In Switzerland, he had already been told, he would go to a Swiss school. Americans would be few and far between.

At first, things worked out. The name "Woodrow" had no associations for the children and none of them had heard of Woodrow Wilson. All the double-ues intimidated them. They were comfortable with "Wudi" and so was he. Had it not been for a friend's little sister, that part of his life, at least, would have flowed smoothly.

The sister, Elspet, was fascinated by the difficulty of his full name and too young, at eight, to care about failure. It was just too alien, however, and she neither mastered the pronunciation nor remembered the syllables from day to day.

She held Woodrow the person in little reverence, however. From her, he learned the idiom *Du spinnscht—*"you spin" or "you're nuts;" she pointed out this aspect of his character frequently and forcefully. When, at last, she tired of struggling with his name, she decided *Wirbel* was close enough.

He thought nothing of it until it caught on with everyone else. Worrying that it might be a real word, he looked it up. It meant "whirl" or "cowlick." Which was intended, he did not know. The first was connected with spinning, which was something, he had been told, that he did. The other was arguably appropriate too. Neither was good.

Fortunately, he joined the *Pfadfinder* right at that time and needed to recommend a nickname for himself. He knew he must act quickly or *Wirbel* would recommend itself. All would be lost. "Holzli" was an equivalent for "Woody" he had invented one day during a run-in with Elspet.

"Wood is *Holz,* so 'Woody' is just 'Holzli,'" he instructed her.

"*Du spinnscht,*" she informed him. "That is even dumber than your real name—*Wirbel.*"

Nevertheless, it became his Scout name and he did all in his power to promote its general use. Elspet would not use it, but, when he started at the international school, he could say it was his name with a clean conscience. It did not help him make a place for himself, but, he decided in time, nothing would have.

And, at long last, he was not Woodrow.

CHAPTER 6

The Asian assignment had come abruptly, almost before Holzli's mother and he knew that foreign postings were possible. His father seemed settled into administration, though he had joined the Foreign Service with an eye to travel. There was no time to prepare. They all studied Mandarin after their arrival, but it would have been better to hit the ground running. It was long before they outgrew their dependence on fortune—on the chance that others knew English.

Warned, they started German before the fact. Graduate school had given Holzli's father the ability to read about art but little else. He could not speak or hear. They hired a German who had come to learn T'ai Chi. To feed himself, he taught strange English to Chinese children.

The German he gave the Lloyds had its own peculiarities. Herr Blitzer insisted they use a textbook he bought in a stall on the street. Much time was devoted to the sea voyage they might have taken to Europe before the war. They knew what to say at the Captain's table and how to respond to the Captain's invitation to dance. They could say many things about their steamer trunks. To Holzli's disappointment, they skipped the dirigible lesson.

At the same time, they read books about Switzerland. They had had to feel their way into Chinese culture, an entry too painful on balance to repeat. They would meet the new people on less marshy ground.

Holzli bent his energies to a study of *Hornussen* or "Hornets," billed by one author as "the traditional Swiss sport." The descriptions raised doubts—either a titanic joke was being perpetrated or they were moving to the Twilight Zone. The Swiss would fulfill the Chinese' worst suspicions about Westerners. In the end, he pushed thoughts of *Hornussen* deep down where he would not stumble across them.

They flew into Zürich a few days before Christmas, at the decade's midpoint. He had forgotten there was cold like this anywhere on earth or that the air could be so still. Snow had to be relearned.

There was one hotel in the village, tiny, almost hidden in the shadows of the church. They stayed instead in the big town where he later changed from bus to train on his way to Zürich. The hotel there, the Hotel Bahnhof, was a big, white box of a building, trimmed in green, on a corner of the main street.

The roof was its interesting feature, so tall and so sharply sloped on all sides that it was almost a brown tile pyramid. Dormer windows peeked out of it, and Holzli would have given much to know what rooms were there and how shaped. His own room was on the second floor of four, just above the restaurant.

The owner was P. Manzo-Schumacher. Whether he was Swiss from the south or genuinely Italian was never clear. Each night Italian voices penetrated the floor and swelled in power till late. Choruses of "Santa Lucia" marked the end— when they started, Holzli knew there were thirty minutes left at most.

His family ate in the restaurant mornings and evenings. Breakfast was bread and rolls with marmalade and butter. He could have a sort of cereal called *Müesli* if he wanted. The marmalade was full of puzzling sticks.

For dinner they had what the restaurant decided to serve. There were always pommefrites, whatever else was offered. The main course was wienerschnitzel more and more consistently once the staff discovered that he liked it. His parents were not as partial to it but they had no say. After experimentation, he settled on Linzertorte as his regular dessert.

Apfelsaft was another find—apple cider bottled like wine and sparkling. He preferred it to alcohol, which seemed counterproductive by the thirst it caused. This provoked his first authentic, extended use of German. On Christmas Eve, he was handed a glass of eggnog by their host and drained off half before tasting something wrong. He coughed in protest.

"But it's *real* eggnog," his mother said. "Real eggnog has brandy in it. What you're used to is only a part of the whole."

He could not have said why this shook him as it did. Part of his life had been a lie, and now he knew it.

"How do you like it?" she asked.

Herr Manzo-Schumacher did not speak English but seemed to understand the question and share it. His face was all query.

"*Es schmeckt mir gut,*" Holzli told him. "*Aber es macht mich durstig.*"

The host and a waitress who stood by treated this as genius, but, again, he tasted something false. Had he botched it? He decided he did not care—he had communicated his point, and that was his only standard of success.

Next door and attached was the Cinema Manzo. An older Manzo-Schumacher ran it. It showed German or American movies except on Saturday afternoons, which, as Holzli found out, were given to Italian films.

They saw *The Roots of Heaven* there one night, which his parents had seen years before when it first came out. He noticed posters in the narrow lobby advertising a Western.

"But not in English," his father pointed out. "The Winnetou books were written by a German and this is part of a series of movies they're making based on them. In German. I read something about it just recently."

"That doesn't matter," Holzli protested. "How am I going to learn German if I don't listen to it?"

"And you know they don't let children into all movies here," his mother put in.

He knew. It was a sore point. "We don't know this is one of them."

"Intelligent policy, too," his father said. "Need to do more of that in the States. Look, it doesn't matter to me one way or the other if you go see it. I just don't want you wasting your time or being disappointed. Talk to Mr. Manzo. See what he says."

It was best, Holzli judged, to assent to this, but he had no intention of talking to the Manzo intended. That Manzo might say something to derail things immediately. The signs under the posters said, as best as Holzli could tell, that the Winnetou movie was Saturday at two. He would show up then and confront the elder Manzo, who seemed friendlier than his relative—and more diffident.

It did not go as smoothly as it should have. The man did not want to let him in and kept explaining something Holzli could not understand. His few weeks' experience had been enough to teach him, however, that this was to his advantage. It was often useful, in fact, to feign bewilderment when you grasped things perfectly. This must be the problem about his age, and the problem might go away if it could not be conveyed.

He won when the line behind him grew long enough. Inside, he took a seat far to the side where he would be least evident. Soon, the projector began to clatter and the screen lit up.

The coming attraction featured people driving around Rome in sports cars. This was fine with Holzli—he was mildly fond of sports cars since seeing *Goldfinger*. Though this was starting to drag on a bit long, he felt fortunate to be in the theater watching it at all.

After fifteen minutes, he began to worry. What could this be? A short feature? He had seen no such thing in American theaters since he was small. He strained to remember if the posters suggested a double feature.

Thirty minutes in, he conceded that this must be a movie. He relaxed and let the flood of dapper men and stylish women wash over him. He could tread water until the second feature.

He overestimated himself. Nothing happened in this film but conversations in apartments and restaurants and traffic. Lulled by the Italian, he started to drowse, and, in his drowsing, the language grew intelligible. He could understand the actors. They were saying nothing significant but they seemed to say it coherently.

He never fell entirely asleep and, at long last, the credits crawled glacially up the screen. Climbing aback to consciousness, he stretched and sat up expectantly. When the film stopped, however, the lights came up and the theater emptied. He remained where he was, though his hopes died by the second.

A throat cleared behind him. He turned his head to see the Manzo in the doorway to the lobby, looking sad. That was all there was to be. Holzli thanked the man and went back to his room.

The room was always cold. He sat layered in outdoor clothes with his feet next to an electric heater, or took long baths. A huge, white cloud of a comforter, like a giant pillow, bigger than the mattress, made the bed another haven. He used the inside windowsill, behind the curtains, as a refrigerator.

His parents' room was warmer when they first arrived because his mother insisted on getting a Christmas tree. One hung the tree with white candles here instead of colored bulbs, and the heat given off was gratifying. If the concept of dry pine needles decked with open flame had not raised such questions with them, the tree would have stayed alight for the two months they lived there.

Most of their presents were little enough to fit into luggage. Holzli's favorite among those he received was local, actually, but similarly small. It was a type of pocket-knife used by the Swiss army, like nothing he had ever seen in the U.S. Red with a white cross on it, like the flag, it was not limited to blades—all manner of tools folded out of it.

The hotel staff harassed him with the claim that he had missed Samichlaus, who had been by with gifts on the sixth. This was, charitably considered, funny the first couple of times.

Sometimes he would ride the tiny elevator to the basement with a pocketful of *Franken*. A coin-operated bowling alley was there, a meter and a half wide, with balls like croquet balls and pins proportional.

For the rest, in those early weeks, he read Ian Fleming and walked about the town.

When school started up again in the village, his mother drove a tunnel of snow to bring him in and pick him up. The schedule of full days and half days and holidays changed weekly, so this did not always work out well. Sometimes he waited a morning for classes to begin, and sometimes no one came at all.

There was a printed schedule, it turned out, which Herr Ehrlich was not giving him. When the other students learned that he was not getting a copy, someone would give him his own each week, bringing it from home where it arrived by mail.

His first day was a hell of incomprehension and isolation. His mother and he were met by the head of the school, who had some English, and taken to meet Herr Ehrlich, who beamed at his mother like a full moon. Then the teacher and he left for the classroom, and he understood nothing more that day.

When and where he was told to sit, he sat. When they changed rooms, he followed along to find that they had singing practice. When others opened their books, he peeked to see the page number and he sang the words phonetically, careful to wait until the others started each note before matching it and raising his voice.

Books and green, gridded notebooks had been waiting on his desk that morning. In New Jersey, the desks had empty holes where inkwells once fitted. Here, the holes were filled. Inside the notebooks were rectangles of fuzzy paper he could not identify.

Only when Herr Ehrlich wrote on the board could Holzli tell what topic they were covering. He copied everything that went up in order to bring something away, since the spoken words meant nothing to him.

While he was copying multiplication tables, intent on this task, the teacher suddenly stopped talking. Holzli took no notice until the quiet had such strength it could not be ignored. He looked up.

Herr Ehrlich's face was glowing red as though he were holding his breath. His eyes were clamped on Holzli's hand, which held a ballpoint pen. The boy could not interpret what was happening or imagine what he should do, so he froze in mid-stroke.

Before Holzli noticed it was moving, the teacher's hand came down, flat palmed, on the surface of the nearest girl's desk. The crash brought the girl to her feet to avoid going over backwards. Her chair clattered to the floor.

Again too swiftly to register, Herr Ehrlich was right before him and snatched the pen from his hand so forcibly it flew across the room to click against a window. The teacher began to speak in a low, steady voice with a rhythm that slammed the syllables against the boy. When he was finished, he went calmly to his own desk to bring back another pen—not a ballpoint. He set it on Holzli's desk and gestured at it, smiling.

Holzli never gave the pen back, not knowing if he was meant to. It was two parts, a wooden shaft and a point that slid into it. He learned not to leave a trail of ink from the inkwell to the paper, and he learned that the fuzzy rectangles were blotters.

Some of his work differed from his fellows' in the Fourth Class. He was given a chart of cursive letters and told to change his handwriting to match it. He needed to remember to do ones and sevens and double-esses properly. On the reading side, he was far behind the others in deciphering the Gothic script of half their reading assignments.

Gym class was the brightest spot in each day since it was hard to misunderstand what was wanted. The school's gymnasium was so well appointed that they never got around to using much of the equipment. Typically, the most exotic and fun-looking equipment, the function of which he was dying to know, went idle.

They played *Fussball,* or soccer, on a lot between the school and the butcher shop. Soldiers on active duty drilled there, but *Fussball* practice had priority. When the children came out, the soldiers stacked their Sturmgewehr57 assault rifles around the border of the field and disappeared somewhere for the duration.

"Do we ever play *Hornussen?*" Holzli asked Paul, Elspet's brother, one day in the gymnasium.

"Hornets? Is that an American game?"

"No, it is Swiss, I think."

Paul shook his head. "I have never heard of it."

CHAPTER 7

Cold and dark came quickly now and it did not do to linger. Still, one could not let nature determine everything. Holzli wanted to visit Franz Carl Weber's to see what was new among the magic tricks and practical jokes on the lowest floor. Mark again could not or would not go, but Konrad's parents were out of town and his time was freer.

The year was far enough along that chestnuts were roasted and sold on the corners. Konrad bought a bag; Holzli wanted to reserve his money against happy finds at the store.

"But give me a *bitzeli*," he said to Konrad.

"You are becoming Mark, maybe," Konrad responded. However, Holzli was given some chestnuts.

Here in the narrow, ancient streets and alleys, where little traffic went, it was almost silent. Near the center of the block, they could hear, for a moment, a radio through a window that could not be open in this weather. "Sunny Afternoon," a recent favorite of Holzli's, by the Kinks. He started to hum, caught in its current, and felt off-balance when it cut off in the middle of a phrase.

"Don't say I'm turning into Mark! I have more than enough of my own problems."

"Of what sort?"

"Nothing I want to talk about."

Konrad's lips tightened into a straight line. They did this often; Holzli had decided this was Konrad's notion of a bitter smile.

"Why is your mouth twitching this time?" he asked.

The other seemed to consider whether to take offense and decide against it. "You are not Mark, then, in that way. He never does not want to talk about his problems."

"Is he having more auras?"

"That and other things. He is telling me more stories like the one I told you before. And he complains that he cannot talk to his family about them. They will assume he is crazy."

"Well..."

"Do not say it. It is too obvious a joke to make. You are too predictable now be funny."

Now Holzli had to deliberate whether to be offended.

"Okay," he said finally. "What are the new stories? The last one was a month ago and he hasn't seemed much different from usual. It can't be bothering him that much."

"Mark is the way he is because he is always very bothered by everything. He would only change if he were suddenly not bothered."

Holzli mirrored Konrad's bitter smile. "What are the new stories?"

"Let me see if I can tell them well. They have details that I need to remember and tell in order. There are two incidents and I do not want to mix them up."

Away from the lake and the river, the wind was stopped by buildings, each street of structures another hedge in its path. The cold did not stab as it could along the water.

"The first happened on the Gstadstrasse again, at the same place in Zollikon as the one last month—the house with the plaque. The second was just recently, in town along the Limmat.

"He was going home again a couple of weeks ago. He had not taken the uphill route since that one day—he always went downhill from the Dufourstrasse and did not have to go near that house. He was afraid of it.

"But he knew he was afraid of it, so he was ashamed. So, of course, he finally went there.

"Everything happened just as before. This time, he thought to try to get away but worried that...well, I guess that he would get lost if he moved. That is what I think he was telling me. That he was actually going somewhere when things changed and he should not leave the point where he entered.

"It was all more sharp—sharper—this time. More intense. Especially, he could smell the animals. The manure from the animals. He said he could see part of the courtyard through a little open gate and he could not tell what was mud and what was from cows and horses. And the smell of piss was sharp."

"This was his vision? I can believe it of Mark, I guess, but..."

"I am just telling it the way he told me. The point is that everything was sharper and clearer to him. He was more there.

"He could hear more, too. Someone was yelling a street or two over, but he could not tell what it was about. There were not many people on his own street. He says they were dressed like people from the past..."

This was too much to endure. "That's the giveaway! That's what his stories are leading to! I see it now. This is just like his U.F.O. story, but it's supposed to be about time travel. Make him tell more about the clothes—he'll screw it up!"

"He *did* describe them, sort of. Do you want to hear the rest of this or not?"

"Were they wearing lederhosen?"

"Do you want to hear this?"

As little as Holzli was willing to grant Mark, deep in some trench in the floor of his soul he wanted Mark to be honest and sane in this. Months before, when Mark was claiming to see a flying saucer enter the lake late each night, it was not easy to pretend to believe him. Yet, Holzli had done it, fearing that the storyteller would abandon his tale. If that happened, all hope in its truth would be gone. When it did happen, the part of Holzli that wanted an alien base under the lake was crushed. He was no longer willing to play along with this sort of thing. But he was not so calloused that he would not listen if the story was offered.

"Okay, go ahead. I'll shut up."

"He said the clothes were 'floppy.' At first, he saw only men and they had very loose clothes that overlapped a lot."

His listener wrinkled his forehead at him in puzzlement.

Konrad shrugged. "I do not know. They also had big belts. And some had big hats with wide brims, though one had a sort of Wilhelm Tell affair with a feather. Anyway, it all added up to 'floppiness.' He did say that they wore tights, but they had floppy boots almost up to the knee."

"He thinks they were farmers—they carried rakes and things and they were covered with mud or something. Nothing looked exactly like anything in our Swiss history book, but it was all work clothing, so it would not. Oh, many had these deals over their shoulders like American Pilgrims. I do not know what that is supposed to look like."

"But then he saw women?"

"No, a girl. Her clothes did not help either. Let me tell this in order, though.

"As I say, he was afraid to move, so he just stood at the edge of the road. He was nervous about anyone coming close to him since he could not step away. He did not look like these people and they seemed rough—and they carried things they could turn into weapons.

"For a while, there was no real danger. No one came toward him or looked in his direction. He watched them intently."

"He did what?"

"He watched them very carefully. He tried not even to make small movements so he would not draw attention. He wanted to sneeze from the dust in the air, but he fought that down.

"A couple of the men passed each other and exchanged acknowledgements."

"Did Mark really use words like that or are you just showing off?"

"So, then, you do *not* want to hear this."

Holzli shook his head. "I said nothing of the sort. Tell it however you want."

The German boy stopped and looked around. "Wait, is this the right way?"

"Yes, we just have to wind through there." He pointed to the opening to a tight and twisted alleyway between two walls.

"This is not the way I have come."

"Just trust me. Go on with the story."

"*Jawohl, mein Führer*! Well, then, to continue: He was watching one of these meetings and did not notice a man coming up behind him until he heard steps. He whirled around—the man was only three meters or so away.

"Mark jumped and nearly screamed. Then he quickly worked up a smile and got ready to greet the man. But the man was not looking at him. He passed right by without looking.

"It was too strange. It was not as though the man was ignoring him—Mark felt that the man did not see him at all. Maybe he *could* not see him. He believed this as soon as he thought of it: no one else seemed to notice him and he would appear very odd to them.

"He was too shaken to test this on the man who had passed, but soon he had another chance. Another person came by, and Mark *grüezi*ed him and waved. The man did not turn his eyes or change his speed. There was no reaction at all."

This is very, very good, Holzli thought. Too good for Mark to make up? What about Konrad? Konrad was smart but he had little imagination. He had chosen his mother's stolidity and pale blonde hair over his father's dark playfulness. Eberhard Müller might fabricate such things in fun, but his son would not. Sarcasm was the limit of Konrad's invention.

"This gave Mark confidence, and, when the girl we are talking about came along, he thought he was invisible.

"She was perhaps nine or ten years old. She turned into the farmhouse's courtyard before she got to him but she was not in there long. When she came out, she continued in his direction.

"So, we have Mark thinking he is invisible, and this girl headed toward him who, he remembers later, is walking with her head down, not watching where she is going. At the last minute, he steps out of the way, automatically, to keep from being bumped. The girl would keep on down the road, never noticing him, but he grunts when he moves.

"She looks up at him. Her eyes open almost as wide as her mouth."

"I would have screamed and screamed if looked up and saw... "

"Remember what I said about predictable humor. What is important is that she sees him. She does, as a matter of fact, gasp, and then so does Mark.

"She has many layers of clothing too, with an apron on top of it all. Her head is wrapped in a scarf. To Mark, this just looks like an old-fashioned costume—he cannot tell anything from it.

"She is not afraid. However, she is confused by him. Tactfully, she asks, 'What are those clothes?'

"Mark cannot think of a helpful answer. 'Just clothes,' he says. He cannot think of much at all. He has someone who might help him understand what is happening to him and he cannot come up with any questions.

"'Who are you?' is the best he can do.

"'I am Regula Schneider,' she tells him.

"Nothing occurs to him to follow with.

"'And who are you?' she asks."

"Wait, wait," demanded Holzli. "This is all taking place in German?"

Konrad stopped with his mouth open. "I did not even think of that!"

"Because Mark doesn't..."

"...know much German at all," Konrad finished for him. "Though they did not say anything complicated."

"Still, it's more than Mark can handle. This is our proof—the whole thing's a lie."

"I am afraid you are right. I had not even thought about it. You are not half as stupid as everyone says. Not one third, perhaps."

"Forget about the rest of the story. Here's the store, anyway. Why does he do these things?"

CHAPTER 8

About the middle of February, the World Council of Churches, meeting in Geneva, called for a cease-fire in Vietnam. The next day, Muhammad Ali was reclassified 1-A.

Geneva was in that otherworldly part of Switzerland where French was spoken. That realm touched Holzli only faintly and in the least and strangest details: one could thank someone with *merci vielmal* if one did not labor at the *merci*. He did not think of the southern city as local—the Council might as well have met in Paris.

Graubünden, reported to be linguistically bizarre on another order of magnitude, he was yet to visit. He felt no more identity with that canton than with Geneva. News from neither drew his interest especially. When Peggy Fleming won a gold medal in Davos, it did not register with him. When the boys in the village congratulated him, he had only the vaguest notion why. He decided the victory drew their attention because of its setting, and he felt nothing for that setting.

For the same reason, he thought, the Council's appeal fixed the boys' awareness on the war. Holzli's mind had brushed over it in the *Herald Tribune* and let it pass. His friends' questions irritated him since he had no desire to discuss the issue. His father and the year in Virginia had exhausted him.

The school in Virginia held three kinds: the native Southerners, the children of federal employees, and the odd politician's son or daughter. At least, this held abstractly. For significant purposes, these groups ran together in an undifferentiated mass, melted in love of Lyndon Johnson.

His father's position made Holzli one of these—one of the loyal dependants of the Administration. Still, he had lived elsewhere and, by the minor grace of that, was not quite what the others were. Smug and closed and somehow rural in their limitations, these children of Washington, living almost in the nucleus of power, might have grown up in cornfields a thousand miles away for all that he could see.

Since he believed what they believed, it was hard for him to say how they differed. He told himself, finally, that he supported the Great Society and the war because reason led him that way. They did not have that ground: they believed what everyone else believed because everyone else believed it.

Their families' incomes played a part too. That, he felt, was contemptible.

His father worked for the same people, but that could never bend his own thoughts.

He tried to discuss things with his classmates and found this was a mistake. Arguing for ideas he knew they held implied that argument was necessary—that other views were possible. It did not win him friends.

At home, his father would, with no pattern, lecture him on the same topics. This just bored him. He tried to find the signs that these lessons were coming. Warned, he could have hidden. They were not arguments that spoke to him—father and son reached the same places from different directions.

He learned not to let this show. It brought mockery.

"You think anyone is for or against the war with any conviction? Watch. Watch what happens if we need more soldiers and really try to draft the middle class. *Then* you'll see an anti-war movement. What exists now is nothing and can do nothing.

"And then watch what we do if that movement throws us out of power. If the Republicans take over running the war, we'll be against it. We'll *always* have been against it as far as the public remembers. I might switch parties at that point—I don't know. Things will change hands again and partisan loyalty looks good. Over time, either party will do."

After Taiwan, Holzli could not even meet his father at the same endpoints. They shared neither starting places nor destinations. This came on Holzli delicately and slowly, by the tiniest deflection of his thoughts on the subtlest of levels.

As they would in Switzerland, they lived in a hotel in Taipei on first arriving, before they could find an apartment. The nightstand in Holzli's room held two books, huge and tiny. The big one was a telephone directory. The other had been left by the Endowment for Pneumatic Development.

This introduced itself on the back cover: "Endowment for Pneumatic Development is funded group puts books in rooms to foster harmonic appreciation of traditional literatures. Please to free to take the copy."

The book itself was called the *Way Virtue Classic,* and Holzli did make off with it. He liked the way it looked, hard-covered in fake red leather with embossed gold letters. The pages were thin almost to transparency, and the print was muddy, but the whole was neat and heavy and compact and felt good in his hand.

He could not tell how many of his problems with the text were due to the translation. Much was trackless for him, whatever the cause. Yet, the very language, tortured and dark, fascinated him and pulled him through each little section to the end.

"What's that you've got there?" his father asked, passing through the living room of the new apartment. A month after the move, their belongings had arrived from the States. Holzli had begun to organize his books and searched out the hotel book to slot it in with the others. Finding it in an unpacked bag, he had opened it, charmed again by its surface and heft, and walked absently into the living room, reading.

"One of those books from the hotel rooms."

"Books from the hotel rooms?"

"They were in the drawers by the beds. In my room, anyway."

"I suppose I never looked." The man's mind leapt to the association natural to it. Holzli was experienced enough to catch the moment in his father's face. "You just took it from the room?"

"You were supposed to. It says to. Look, here on the back."

The boy handed the volume over to his father, who read the cover and laughed. He opened it and thumbed the pages till the book fell open of itself.

"'Govern country by rectitude,'" he read aloud. "'War by craftiness. But gain world by do nothing.'"

He looked up at his son, holding the page with his finger. "Who translated this—Charlie Chan?" A puff of air through his nose, which Holzli took for a laugh, made the free page jump.

"Let's see. 'How do I know this? By this: More prohibitions in world, poorer people. More knives and swords people have, more disorder country is. More skilled clever people, more unpredictable things rise. More regulations and laws are promulgated, more thieves and robbers.

"'Therefore, sage say:'"—his face twisted and his voice turned sing-song—"'I do nothing, and people reformed on own. I devote self to quietude, and people justice on own. I not meddle, and people wealthy on own. I have no desires, and people honest on own.'"

He tapped the page three times rapidly. "You know, this is just the *Tao Te Ching*." He turned the book over and reread the title. "I must have a good translation of this somewhere. I'll lend it to you."

"You don't need to. This one is good enough for me." That sounded too weak—it might still invite the replacement. "I like it."

"I'll look for the other one. I have to say, though, that the author seems to miss the point."

He looked at Holzli as though awaiting a response, but his son said nothing. "You know?" he prodded.

Already, they had learned to swim in the sea of noise from outside and the other apartments—the voices, car horns, music, and fireworks. In silences, however, it flooded in.

"No, I don't know what you mean," Holzli said, finally.

"He doesn't seem to know why he should want government to begin with. Why do states exist at all? It can't just be to keep things peaceful and prosperous—that's fine for livestock but not for human beings."

He was silent once more and the sea poured in again while the boy waited for enlightenment.

There was nothing further. The father tilted his head in the way he had when he marshaled his words, but then he turned and walked from the room. He left the book on top of others in the bookshelves near the door.

Holzli retrieved it and laid it on the desk in his room, the top of which was still mostly bare. He did not return to it for days and, when he did, it was gone. In its place was the promised substitute. He never saw his own copy again, even after thorough, secret searches in his father's territories.

CHAPTER 9

"I don't know how we talked. I didn't say it was in German. We just talked like you and me are doing now. Like we were talking English. I didn't think how funny that was till later, either."

Konrad was angry enough with Mark to confront him at the lunch break and he brought Holzli with him to flaunt the broken confidentiality.

"Why did you tell Holzli?" Mark whined in moist outrage.

"Do not try to deflect this back to me," said Konrad. "I was willing to listen to your bullshit because I thought you, at least, believed it. Whether it was real or not. Maybe you needed help. I am the one who is betrayed."

"It's not a lie! I don't know how we talked! Nothing about this makes sense—it's not my fault, it's just the way it is."

An explosion of tears waited for a trigger, so Holzli decided to supply it. "Why should we believe this after that flying saucer crap?"

The explosion came. "I don't *care* whether *you* believe it, you asshole!" Mark did not look at Holzli. He turned his head so they would not see him cry. His nose had begun to run almost at once.

Holzli thought again of the slugs, formlessly soft and mucous. It hurt him, somehow, and he wished he had not spoken.

"Please...I'm sorry," he said. "I don't know whether it's true or not. I just had this question about what language you were using."

The lie put Konrad in a bad position, isolating him as the bully, and he glared reproachfully at Holzli.

It was too late, however—Holzli was trapped in a sympathetic role. "Can I hear the rest of the story?"

They were in a corner of the garden, not far enough from other students to go unobserved. Holzli glanced over to see a quartet of chemical people—a boy and three girls—smirking at them.

Mark himself was oblivious. He sniffled and ran the back of his hand across his nose. "What...how much did Konrad tell you?"

Holzli perceived that Konrad's part had shifted onto him. He was the confidant now. He did not like it. Yet, he felt bad at the boy's distress and could not harden himself against him.

He summarized. Konrad walked away. Planned or not, it was exquisite vengeance, cementing Holzli's fate.

Mark took up the tale. "I told her my name, but there wasn't much more I could say. I didn't know what would mean anything to her. She thought there was something wrong about me. That I was crazy. She wasn't scared I'd hurt her, but she was nervous like I would follow her around and embarrass her or be hard to get rid of."

"That Rat Fink patch on your coat may not have helped."

"I wasn't wearing that!" Mark had not, in fact worn the coat more than once in Holzli's memory—its reception at school had been painful to witness. "You're right that my clothes were a problem. But I couldn't let her get away.

"I asked her whose house that was she'd visited.

"'Oh, that's Mr. Thomann's,' she told me. 'I wanted to see if my father was there. He wasn't.'

"She looked me up and down and I could tell she was starting to think I wasn't just strange but funny. Comical. She was getting a look in her eye like a laugh. But she still didn't want me around.

"'I still have to find him,' she said, and she was turning to leave.

"'Wait!' I said. My voice broke and I was loud. It startled her. She began to walk away.

"'Where is this place?' I called. Too loud again, but I didn't want to run after her—that would be worse.

"She answered, 'Zollikon!' over her shoulder. She had an amazed look on her face.

"I stuttered, 'But...but...'"

"She stopped about fifty feet from me. She said, 'What do you want?'

"I tried to talk and was just stuttering again. Then the funny feeling and the lights came. The last thing I saw before it got too bright was her face—and now she really was scared. I don't know what she saw, but, even if I just disappeared into thin air, it, well..."

"Her curiosity may have been tickled." If Holzli had to fill in for Konrad, he might as well have appropriate lines.

"Well, more than that!"

"I know, I know. It was a joke." If the story was true, it was hideously unfair that Mark was the one chosen by whatever powers might be. Holzli could think of no one less suitable for adventure of any profundity. More grounds it could not be true.

"That wasn't the end, though, right? Konrad says something else happened by the river."

"Yeah! A lot more happened." Mark's tearfulness had vanished in the excitement of the telling. "I can't stand to be around my family anymore, now that this has started happening. I feel weird about it and it might make me act weird. I can't tell. But that makes me act weird by itself. Or, anyway, I keep thinking my parents or brother think I'm acting weird, so they make me jumpy.

"Every chance there is, I try to get out of the apartment. Mostly, I just walk around Zollikon or go north to town. Last Saturday, I just went up past school along the water. I was sort of headed toward the Lindenhof, but that was only to have a place to walk to. I stayed on this side past the Quai Bridge because I decided to poke around the Grossmünster, the big church. When I got there, though, I just looked at the panels on the bronze doors for a while.

"I almost crossed the bridge there but changed my mind—there are antique stores on a street a little further up and it's fun to look in the windows. I didn't do that either, though. What I ended up doing is going to look at the river at this place they have by the next bridge up. It's a kind of platform they have that sticks out into the water almost straight across from the Lindenhof.

"And then the lights started again. It hadn't happened before outside of Zollikon. I didn't think it would. I don't feel safe from it anywhere anymore."

He did not sound as disturbed as Holzli would expect, however. Another reason to hold these narratives at arm's length?

"This time, there were people all around, in all kinds of clothes. They didn't look like medieval people—they looked later. It was *really* crowded. Everyone was trying to push toward the river. We weren't on the platform I'd been on. There were stalls all around, but I didn't look to see what was in them. All the people were looking across the river, so that's where I started looking too.

"And because I was doing that, trying to make out who on the other side they were watching, it was a minute or two before I noticed something. I turned my head a little, and this woman's face was right next to mine. I mean really close. Really, really close. When I jumped back, I didn't bump into anyone, which was odd, but I wasn't paying attention to that because I saw something odder: the woman's shoulder had been *in* me! The woman hadn't been behind or in front of me! We'd been standing in the same place!

"And I looked around and now I was standing in a man! I got spooked and backed away really quickly, but that just meant I was backing through more people. There wasn't anything I could do except go for it and run through the crowd..."

"So to speak," contributed Holzli.

"What?"

"Sorry, never mind. But it goes along with no one being able to see you before."

"Except Regula."

"Yeah, but no one else. Did anyone notice you this time?"

"Not yet. I'm getting to that."

"Could you touch *things?*"

Mark considered. "I don't know. I could touch one person, but I'm getting to that."

"Hey! You could touch the ground, right? You didn't sink into the ground."

"I guess so," the other conceded without apparent interest.

"And you could breathe air, right?"

"I guess so."

"And *see*. Light's sort of physical, I think...And sound uses air..."

Mark seemed to have tired of responding.

"So, what happened then?"

"Well, I was heading toward the edge of the crowd. Going pretty fast. And I ran into someone. I went down backwards and hurt my wrist—I put out my hand behind me to break my fall. It felt strained but it's okay now."

"So you *could* touch the ground."

"I guess so." He still manifested no real interest. "No one was worried about me, of course, but they all gathered around the girl I ran into. They helped her up and dusted her off. She was trying not to cry. It was Regula!

"They were asking if she was all right and what happened."

In German? Holzli suppressed the question.

"She would have seen me except she wasn't looking around. Her dress was dirty and torn at the side near her knee and she was fiddling with that. I got some people in between us in case she raised her eyes.

"She couldn't tell them what happened, and there was nothing serious wrong with her, so they turned toward the river again. Everyone was interested in something on the other side. Even Regula—she forgot about her dress pretty quick when the crowd started murmuring. Something new was going on over there.

"I could barely see anything with everyone shifting around, so I sneaked over behind Regula. It wasn't till I was close that I noticed something. Her clothes were different, of course, but the same kind. What I noticed different is that she was older than she'd been. About our age. You could tell from her face. It was...bonier. No, not bonier, but it had more shape.

"And she was filled out a little here." He made vague cupping gestures around his chest. "But she wasn't much taller than she'd been. She was still smaller than me."

Holzli snorted despite himself. The mention of smallness might not be incidental. Konrad and he had many speculative and querulous discussions of the difference in growth between the boys and girls in their class. The girls towered over the boys. They hunched their shoulders in self-consciousness, as humiliated by their heights as the boys by their deficits, but this just made them loom. Mark was infatuated with a girl named Vicki White who was tallest of all. One could almost follow every dimension of her growth day by day. This, plausibly, then, was Mark's imagination entirely. A Vicki short and manageable, not tall and intimidating. Should this be the case, Holzli had access to his classmate in a way and at a level he did not like.

Again, he thought of slugs. Once, while walking with some boys from the village on a hillside near his house, he had seen something he could not come near to recognizing. About twelve centimeters long, pale, mottled and tumorous, it twisted aimlessly and ceaselessly upon itself like a glistening piece of muscle torn from an animal and flung writhing on the ground.

"*Schnecke,*" one of the boys pronounced after examining it with horror in his face.

Holzli did not want to imagine how that could be a slug. They were seeing what should not be on the surface.

"'Regula,' I said, real low so it wouldn't startle her. It was so low, actually, that she didn't hear me at all. 'Regula,' I said louder. 'Don't turn around.' I didn't want her to see me until I could talk to her a bit.

"She turned around and recognized me right away. I could tell she was kind of scared but more just shocked. More than that, I saw...I guess you would call it wonder.

"I didn't keep her from seeing me, but I tried warning her again: 'Don't talk to me! Don't show that you see me! No one else can see or hear me!'

"'It's you!' she said, whispering with big eyes.

"I begged her to turn around. I felt like grabbing her shoulders and doing it myself, but I thought that would frighten her to death. 'Please,' I said, trying to look really worried so she'd know I wasn't going to hurt her.

"'What are you?' she asked.

"I gave up and walked around behind her toward the river so she'd face the right way. She did follow me around.

"'Act like I'm not here,' I told her. 'Talk low like you're talking to yourself and don't look at me. Or they're going to think you're nuts. No one else can see me—I've tested that out.'

"'It has been two years.' She still had wonder all over her. 'You vanished in light so shining I could not look. I knew then you were not a human. I did not tell anyone—I did not know if I should, and no one would believe me anyway. I thought you would be back.'

"'Well, I am.' Like last time, I knew I could be getting information but I couldn't figure out what to ask. 'It's only been a couple weeks for me.'

"I wanted her to know I *was* human. I wanted to be able to talk to her. Maybe if I showed her I didn't know anything, it would help. Once I decided to do that, questions were easy to come up with all of a sudden.

"'What's happening here?' I asked. I moved next to her side so I could see.

"She turned to me and said, 'It is Felix Manz,' and stopped as though this explained everything.

"So I go, 'Who is Felix Manz and what's he doing?' She looked confused, and I said, 'Look, I don't know anything. I don't even know where I am or why I'm here.' The first wasn't exactly true, but it wasn't the Zürich I knew.

"'What are you?' she asked me again. She was looking me in the eyes. I hadn't paid attention before but now I noticed that she had those blue eyes you see on blonde girls around here. She had this sort of dark, reddish-brown hair, though. It was wrapped up again, but you could tell."

Holzli did not like the trajectory. The narrator paused, snared by a picture in his memory or imagination. Holzli tried to jump in, but the window was not open long enough.

"She had these pink splotches on her cheeks like you don't see on American girls.' Mark halted, again too briefly. "And pink lips too."

Brutality was called for. "What did you tell her?"

"What? Oh, I told her my name. I told her how old I was because I figured she was about twelve too. It turned out later she's eleven. I was going to tell her more but I started to think how much I'd have to explain and it seemed too complicated. Things were happening—there wasn't time."

"She was eleven? She sounds older."

"Margaret Owens started filling out last year when she was eleven. You weren't here then."

Margaret Owens was one of the four in the garden with them, no longer observing them and, thankfully, too distant to hear them. Holzli noted that Margaret was focused on the boy in the group, the perpetual pitcher in the baseball games. Her gaze only wavered when the bell rang the end of lunch and all had to go in.

CHAPTER 10

Their house above the village was not finished when they moved in. A giant bunker of concrete, two stories high plus an attic, it was being built for the ages and could not be rushed. The first few weeks, a web of scaffolding wrapped the house for workers to climb and cling about the walls. Any time of day, one might look out a window to find a face beaming back in.

The workers were Italian. They came in the morning, as Holzli set out down the hill to school, and left late. It seemed long but, the first afternoon he stayed home, he saw they had two hours free. They ate enviable lunches, slowly emptying bottles of wine and talking until, on some agreement, they arranged themselves for a short sleep.

One half-holiday, he came home to a gauntlet of diners. Their conversations stopped when he came over a rise in the road, and they watched him without sound or movement till he reached them.

He pulled up *buongiorno* from his memories of the Manzo-Schumachers. It touched off an explosion—immediately, they all rose to their feet and enveloped him in speech, none of which he knew. He got away but never lacked a reception until the house was finished.

It was strange, therefore, to return another afternoon to no response at all. The workers sat stiffly staring at the ground—almost inert, except they chewed their food. The boy examined each as he passed and gathered nothing from any.

When he came to the one he thought of as the foreman, however, the man flicked his eyes up at him, then to the side. It might have been Italian for all that Holzli got from it. The man repeated the gesture and, when Holzli merely stood in wide-eyed blankness, motioned with his chin toward the swimming pool.

This pool was the same concrete as the house, rough and grey as the house's face would always stay, of even depth throughout, with a tiny drain in the center. It was to be filled by a cold-water spigot the size of a bathroom faucet. There was no filter.

They had not filled it and had no certain plans ever to do so. It was a trap for slugs and *Igel*. The latter were either hedgehogs or porcupines—Holzli did not know which. He was not really sure these were two different things and had been too cautious to investigate first-hand. Only one had actually fallen in the pool, and his father had removed it, not he. He stepped aside if he met them on the road in case they could shoot their quills.

He walked to the pool slowly. Nothing good had ever been found in there. As he neared, the far wall was visible over the lip—and something else. What he was seeing did not take form for him for a second, then the uniform and weapon registered. More were visible as he came closer; the pool was full of soldiers in blue-grey wool and green armbands.

Most grinned, and several put their fingers to their lips. One grimaced, however, and waved him away, and the others took that up.

Holzli backed away and composed himself to innocence. He had little doubt what was happening and he could play along. A long stretch of his back, with his arms in the air and a yawn, seemed called for to show ease. While he stretched, he scanned the neighborhood. On the sloping, grassy field beyond the house that ran down to the road along the river was another troop of soldiers. These had red armbands.

He could not see their eyes. They might be staring at him, so he put his palms to his own eyes and rubbed—no one with a pool full of soldiers would concern himself with a headache. If they were not looking, it was a wasted performance, but it cost him little. It made him complicit too and therefore almost military himself.

He was a fan of the Swiss army if not of much else Swiss. It did nothing except litter the *Fussball* field with automatic rifles and damp down the Italians' lunch, but it averted a professional army.

The village was not far from the Rhine, and Holzli had seen the tank traps that still lined the border. A little over twenty years before, they had stood against a genuine threat—and worked.

The armies that flew through Europe and almost crushed Russia could have eaten Switzerland with scarcely a swallow. It would have been a painful swallow, though, for little nourishment. An Alpine fortress of a country, manned by the descendants of soldiers-for-hire, it was not worth the Nazis' while to bother with it. But only, Holzli figured, because the Swiss would never violate their own boundaries. They were neutral in the fullest sense—they did nothing.

The red-banded troops did not invade. He entered the house and watched them from a little window in the attic. One entered the attic by pulling a rope that opened a door in the ceiling, letting a ladder slide down. The window's view took in the grassy slope of undeveloped meadow that gently flattened kilometers into the distance. It made him think of Oz, somehow, especially with its spires on the edge of sight.

The enemy soldiers headed downhill to the road. The boy supposed that the citizen-soldiers' mercenary genes would stand them well in an actual war, but he had no confidence in their peacetime earnestness. It was the *Pfadi* for grownups. For him, as for the Nazis, the Swiss army was important mainly as an abstraction. But there were no American bases in Switzerland and no Swiss forces in Asia.

He climbed down and let the ladder go and the attic shut up on itself. There were yet hours to come of decoding Gothic script and writing out multiplication tables and practicing his new handwriting.

Success in the last was primary since failure would bring the most grief.

Occasionally, he was called upon to read aloud. His phonetic monotone raised snickers, but it passed. The penmanship could not be faked. It was not enough to subdue the habits of years—his old renditions of the letters. Since he was learning elements, he was not allowed a style: his letters must be perfect copies of their models.

Herr Lehrer Ehrlich was having him fill sheets with the same letter. Holzli was never regular enough. His new Z's, large and small, were especially diverse. One day, the week before, he had been sent from the room for a time to work on those. He covered the sheet and sat, postponing judgment, watching the grey clouds gliding north, far away across the Rhine, until he felt he had delayed too long.

"These are the same letter?" Herr Ehrlich's voice cracked. "No! They are not! There is no control here! It is like passing out your *Scheisse* in the street to all who come along!"

The boy was not sure he had heard right. The teacher smiled his smile, the one that conveyed nothing to Holzli in itself but was rarely joined with anything pleasant. However, that day nothing could come of it. Only half that day could be given to real classwork; the rest was for show. The inspectors for the canton were visiting.

Starting after lunch, a man and woman, surprisingly young, visited each class in turn to see them run through their paces. The Fourth Class reran its morning in brief with the same readings and lessons. Holzli did not repeat a reading he had done earlier; he was set to doing math problems. The duo asked questions to test the students after all performances were done—all in High German with stilted responses in kind. Holzli they only asked, in English, how he was enjoying things.

When all classes were sampled, half through the afternoon, everyone assembled in the gym for addresses by the inspectors, school officials and teachers. At first, Holzli sat in strained attention to the words, trying dutifully to follow. His energy failed him and, at length, he slouched back in his chair to wait things out.

It was the Cinema Manzo again. Again he found that semi-consciousness opened all speech to construction. He took significance from everything the speakers said. At intervals, he fought against his drowsiness, propelling himself up to full wakefulness. Then, he knew that the speeches he heard were not the ones delivered. This did not last—he could not keep above the surface, kick as he might. He sank and meaning closed back over him.

At last, he simply slept and, when he woke, everyone was headed though the doors. He jumped to follow but found that the students were scattering as to their homes. They did not dawdle as they would at the end of normal school days, however. They were intent on their destinations.

Were things finished for the day? It was not safe to think so. Were they to come back? Perhaps, but when and why? And what were they supposed to do at home?

He was suddenly too tired even to hunt down someone to ask. For weeks his life had been all inquiry, nothing ever clear or fixed, no course of action obvious, and now he could not bring himself to try anymore. He just went home.

As dark was crawling up from the valley and over the house, someone attacked the front door with fists. Holzli's room was in the downstairs hallway and nearest to the door, but his own door was shut and he had no intention of changing that. He heard his mother answer the knocking and her short exchange with whoever stood outside.

"Woody?" she called when the visitor was gone. "It was Paul. He had bread for you."

"Bread?"

"Do you know what it's about? I couldn't understand most of what he said—it was all Schwyzerdütsch. Open the door."

He came out and was handed a miniature loaf of bread. "What's this for?"

"I said I couldn't tell. It has something to do with school."

"Am I supposed to take it to school?"

"I *said* I don't know."

He did not need another mystery. He moaned, deep in his body, too low for his mother to hear. "I guess I'll find out tomorrow." He threw the loaf onto his desk. It bounced off the wall behind and fell on its side.

"Here," his mother said. "Give it to me and I'll wrap it up. But they can't mean for you to bring it back. We might as well eat it."

"Who knows what they want?" He barely kept below a shout.

"Don't take it out on me. It won't last forever."

He thought she meant the situation, but she might have meant the bread. At any rate, when he asked for it the next morning, she had eaten it.

He cried and got ready for school.

The loaves, he discovered, were a custom. The canton gave them to the children as rewards after each review. For some reason, their delivery had been held up and the students sent home for an hour until they arrived.

Some of the students went through two inspections, though no bread came of the second. Part the curriculum was religious and fitted to a Catholic canton. Reformer children were shipped off to a village down the road for instruction once a week, and these classes, too, were supervised by the canton.

Holzli endured the Catholic lessons as he did all else. He did not care for doctrine. Religion spoke to him through ritual and practice and their effects. The school did not give him those and, these days, he did not get them anywhere else. His father would not go to the village church. They drove to Zürich on Sundays to the big interdenominational church for foreigners.

"It's a matter of which community you want to have a standing in," his father had explained. "Keep this stuff in perspective. The Swiss have it right—religion has its uses in the social order and only there. Everything else is details."

This was dark to Holzli, but, by chance, something happened that was to be taken as illustrative. A friend of theirs, a Dane they had met while living in the Hotel Bahnhof, one day left his wallet on a bus stop bench. Retracing his steps, a full day later, he found the wallet where he had sat.

"I suppose if it had lain there a few days longer, someone would have taken it to the police," he told them. "But that would have inconvenienced me, so everyone who saw it let it lie."

"That's what a good civic religion does for you," Holzli's father commented when they were alone. "It sets invisible guards on things. Guards who can't be tricked or bought or softened."

Holzli did not think that captured the incident. Something was to be said for decency. Still, in Jersey or Virginia or Washington, that wallet would have evaporated like the dew on a summer morning.

Then again, something common ran through this iron integrity and all the little acts that formed these people and marked them off. Cleanliness, perhaps, connected honesty and the compulsive sweeping and washing of walkways. The pervasive quiet that muted even Zürich was a kind of hygiene. But, then, no one ever bathed.

Nor could most things be reduced to simple graciousness or (his father's answer) fear of the beyond.

Maybe pure love of order underlay everything. Holzli knew from his mother's experience with the windows and landlord—and the like stories he swapped with Konrad and Mark—how that love could be reinforced by others if it cooled. Still, where had that love come from?

A couple hours of Gothic reading later—some complaint against the Hapsburgs that would not pull together for him— he went out to check the pool. It was dark. The workers had gone and so, it turned out, had the grey horde. Peace had been restored. He put his palms to his eyes and rubbed. His migraines came without an aura more and more these days.

CHAPTER 11

It had been cold at lunch, but the garden wall cut most of the wind. Afternoon break left them out to be prey to the wind—the younger grades held the garden then. One could stay inside and sit in the library or classroom if one wished. Usually, no one chose that, though Konrad did today.

Holzli and Mark sat over near the kiosk in a circle of trees that opened only to the south. Through the opening, the Alps hung like clouds beyond the lake. Holzli had never noticed them there; perhaps they had never been visible before. He could not remember. Wind came from there also but not at this hour this day.

"'Will you *please* look in that direction and not at me?' I pointed across the river where the quay was as crowded as our side. In fact, this was all one big crowd we were in—the bridge was just as full of people as the docks. On the far side, though, men were making the people move back and clear a space. There was some kind of movement from the bridge onto the quay, but I couldn't see yet what it was.

"I'd thought the river smelled pretty strong but I finally figured out it was fish. There were stalls all along the bridge like the ones near us. It was all a big fish market. Something else was going on, though.

"So, what I told her was that my name was Mark and I was twelve years old and that I wasn't from there. I said I was from a place pretty much like that place but the clothes were different. Then, I thought better and told her I was from Prague."

The whole class had spent a week in Prague just before Holzli transferred in. It was a good call since the girl could well have heard of it. Mark knew the older parts of the city and could talk about them to someone who had almost certainly never been there.

"'But the time is different,' she said. I thought she had caught on to my lie. I just said, 'What?'

"'You said it's only two weeks for you since I saw you outside Mr. Thomann's. There is something wrong with the time. *When* is it for you? What is the date?'

"I was almost in trouble—she was a lot smarter than I wanted. I was getting faster, though, and said, 'What date do *you* think it is?'

"She fell for it. She said it was the fifth of January in 1527. 'Same for me,' I said.

"'Then how is it only two weeks for you?' she asked. I said I didn't know—that I didn't understand anything that was going on. I told her I was hoping she might be able to clear things up.

"That finally loosened her up. She laughed in this really pretty way. Do you know what silver bells sound like?"

Oh, Jesus Christ! thought Holzli. "Yeah."

"She stopped right away—you'll see why. She just forgot for a minute what was happening across the river. Before she could say anything, the noise level really went up. People were turning and telling people behind them something. There was like this slow wave through the crowd.

"A woman in front of Regula turned and said, 'His family is over there. His mother has told him to hold to his faith and not recant. He has said that he will enter the water rejoicing that he can die for truth. He called it a second baptism.'

"I said, 'What in the world?' It wasn't any easier to see things over there. I can tell what I think they did: it looked like they tied a guy's hands together and then made him slip his arms over his knees. Then they put a stick under his knees and over his arms.

"When I looked at Regula, her shoulders were heaving. She was sobbing. It was the first I knew this had anything to do with her. She had just been laughing a minute ago, but I think my being there was making her forget what was going on.

"'So you are not here to save him,' she said. It wasn't a question. It let me know she believed me now—I was just a boy—and that she'd had a reason to hope I was more.

"Neither of us, I guess, could really take this thing in. She was just starting to cry and she'd known about it for a long time. I understood now—sort of—what was being done, but it didn't seem possible.

"'Is that...who did you say it is?' I asked her.

"She couldn't speak very clear but she got out, 'Felix Manz. He is a friend of my father.'

"It was grotesque."

That was one of Holzli's pet words.   Mark had caught it from him. Never had Holzli been able to fit it to a situation so suitably—he did not grudge Mark this use of it.

"'Why are they doing this?" I asked.

"She answered, 'Because he is a Baptizer.' She stopped crying and got this angry expression. Angry and like she decided she didn't care what anyone did to her. 'A Baptizer like my father,' she said. 'And like me.'

"The woman in front gave her a funny look. I don't know what she was thinking, but Regula was too loud.

"I went, 'Shut. Up.' Separately, just like that—I was scared for her. 'They can hear you.'

"The woman's turning around seemed to convince her to keep it down. Whatever, she stopped looking in my direction when she talked.

"She leaned toward me instead so she could whisper, 'I have not seen him since they sent him to the Wellenberg. That tower down there.'

"She nodded to the south.   I could see, way down past the big church bridge, almost where the Quai Bridge is now, a pointed roof and a little bit of the bricks or stones of the building it was the top of. 'That looks like it's right in the middle of the river,' I said.

"Regula said that it was. Manz and another guy, Blue Coat, had been arrested and stuck in there. She had followed earlier that afternoon when he was brought down the river on the side we were on. They took him onto the fish market bridge and read something saying he was being executed for causing trouble and baptizing. Then they took him to the other side. She tried to go too, but the crowd was already too big, so they were stopping people.

"It wasn't just the Wellenberg that was out in the water. Looking both ways, I could see all sorts of things in the river that aren't there now. There were huts and platforms out there up and down the river, and things like fences. The bridges all had buildings next to them.

"Two of them loaded Manz onto a boat and got in with him. Someone on the quay untied the rope and threw it to them and they started out toward our side. But they were going to one of those buildings out in the middle. When they got there, they hauled him out onto the deck of the hut, and each of them held him by an arm right at the edge.

"I couldn't see his face, really. Both me and Regula had to keep moving to see because people in front kept moving. At the end, though, I could tell it was him shouting something.

"'What did he say?' I asked. 'I couldn't understand.' Regula didn't know either, so she asked the woman in front.

"'Sounded like he was chanting Latin,' the woman answered. The man next to her, who was dressed kind of like Henry the Eighth, said that it *was* Latin, and he translated: 'Into your hands, Lord, I commend my spirit.' Then the man said, in this snotty voice, 'They cannot be very serious Reformers if they are still using Rome's tongue.' He made this nasty little smile at Regula. I think he heard what she said before.

"He was so interested in being a shit that he missed it when they dropped Felix Manz in. Manz couldn't move, of course. They held onto him, but his head was under water.

"Remember this was January. The water wasn't frozen but it had chunks of ice floating in it. I was cold myself and I couldn't help imagining what it was like to be that guy, held down under water that cold and not able to move or breathe. I felt like throwing up—I think I almost fainted.

"The two kept him under for a long, long time. After they pulled him out, you could tell he was limp. They laid him on the deck and called back to the other shore, telling them he was dead.

"Some time while all that was going on and I wasn't looking at Regula, she stopped crying. Now, she said, 'I cannot watch any more. I need to leave.'" Mark mimicked her in a dead voice.

"We went around a building she called the Council House and sat down. It was in the same place the old Council House is now but it wasn't the same building. A lot of it was wood. She wanted to go on that side of it because you couldn't see anything from where we sat—no one else wanted to be there.

"'They are going to bring Blue Coat this way now,' she told me, 'so we cannot stay here long. I could not bear it.'

"'Who is Blue Coat?' I asked. 'Is he another Baptizer?' That seemed to be the dangerous thing to be.

"She said, 'He is another friend of my father. They were all together in the New Tower with Mr. Grebel. When they all escaped, those who got away left Zürich. We get messages and money from my father, but he cannot come back. He is really my stepfather—he married my mother when we came here from Einsiedeln.'

"None of this was helping me, but she was saying a lot. Maybe useful things would come out. She was more relaxed while she talked, and I felt good about that. I kept quiet and listened.

"She kept going now that she'd started: 'He is a tailor and he lived in Zollikon. Oh, but you know that. Or not really, but you know I was in Zollikon. I was looking for him at Mr. Thomann's that time because he was helping with the first baptisms.

"'Then Mr. Grebel died of the plague and his father's head was cut off. Mr. Manz and Blue Coat sneaked back in and got caught at a meeting in Grüningen. On the bridge today they said Mr. Manz was being executed because he baptized and taught and was against executions. Blue Coat might get off because he is not a citizen, but no one is sure. We had better leave—I do not want to see him go by.'"

Mark's voice had grown progressively hoarser. He cleared his throat and made experimental noises.

"So you were moving around quite a bit," Holzli commented.

"Yeah, I guess."

"Even though you were afraid to move an inch in Zollikon."

His lips parted as though to speak, Mark slid his eyes to the side, then back to Holzli, then away. "I started moving only because I was startled by being in the same place as other people. After that, it didn't seem to make much difference."

He moistened his lips. "And once I started talking to Regula, I was a lot more comfortable with the whole thing."

Neither spoke. Both stared at the mountains.

"Okay," said Holzli. "Then what?"

"Then we went a little ways up a street, not very far, and sat down. We talked a long time." He was silent again. "We held hands."

"You did not."

"Her mother's family was from Glarus. That's southeast of here. Her grandfather was a barber. Her mother left to go to Einsiedeln with the priest who'd been pastor in Glarus. Einsiedeln is..."

"I've been to Einsiedeln."

"Well, the priest had to go there because of politics. He was too much in favor of the Pope, and the French didn't like that. I didn't understand too much of that part."

He raised his eyebrows at Holzli as though to have it explained. Holzli shrugged.

"He didn't want Regula's mother coming with him, though. He wouldn't have anything to do with her when she followed him. A couple years later, his friends got him a job at the big church here in Zürich.

"People working for the French paid the mother to come to Zürich, and they reported to the town council that the priest had an affair with her. He admitted it but said that she wasn't respectable—she was a slut and a barber's daughter, so it didn't matter. So they gave him the job.

"There wasn't any point in going back to Glarus, so they stayed here in the city. They had the French money to live on for a while. Luckily, Mr. Schneider came along.

"I didn't tell her much about myself. I told her my father was a druggist, which is kind of true. I said I'd lived in Prague all my life and not much had happened to me. She seemed to believe me—she didn't really ask questions. I guess I could have tried to tell her the truth, but I'd already got started on the lie and I wanted her to trust me.

"It was just getting dark when the change came. When I was back, it was still light. It was about the same time as I left here—I don't know exactly what time I left. Maybe no time passed at all."

CHAPTER 12

Swiss television was scheduled like Holzli's school: each broadcast day began and ended at random hours. The content seemed chosen week by week and was perhaps determined by availability. That, at least, was the most popular theory with people Holzli knew—it could not be disconfirmed and it comforted with the possibility of design.

His alternative was the radio. He could pick up two stations from outside. One advertised itself as a "pirate station," and appeared to come from a ship in the North Sea. Its signal was not reliable. The other was the Armed Forces station from some American base in Germany. He preferred the latter for late-night listening, when it listed heavily toward Motown.

It had the advantage, earlier in the evening too, since it was not limited to music. It played old radio shows from the forties and fifties like *The Whistler,* and *Lights Out,* and *X Minus One.* Out of step as Holzli was by now with things Stateside, it did not bother him to be outside its time altogether. If earlier decades could offer him more, he was willing to desert the sixties.

The America in which he touched down on his way to Europe was not the one he had left. Too much was strange— it was almost a new country, replacing the one he had known and leaving him stateless. He had been gone too long and now would be gone longer, and there was nowhere to which he could ever return.

The pirate music was more diverse than the military's, though Nancy Sinatra was ubiquitous and could not be escaped even by switching to local offerings. The pirates were preoccupied, however, with their own status as outlaws and legislative threats to their survival. They liked to play a song called "We Love the Pirate Stations," a plea to be left alone by the British government. Holzli was sympathetic, in a distant way. He trusted political types in general less and less. It must be evidence of the quality of the BBC that anyone went to such trouble to compete with it, he thought, and that confirmed his views on the political temperament. The Armed Forces station itself only fed off the leavings of the private sector.

Unexpectedly, he came into his own music as well. In the bakery one day, sent to buy one of the armored loaves that had become a staple for his family, he was held in conversation by the old woman who waited on customers.

She asked him little questions, then, reaching some decision, asked him to wait while she retreated to whatever rooms backed the shop. There were bumpings back there and the sound of something falling; the door opened again and the woman levered herself back in with a cardboard box in her arms. It was a small collection of Beatles singles, and there was a story, apparently about the woman's niece, that accounted for them. Holzli hated himself for not understanding the explanation, but he could rarely bring himself to ask more questions than urgent need demanded. They were to be his because they were in English.

He did not want the records: there was nothing he could give her in return, and he was too touched by the gift ever to thank her enough. He did his best and left feeling ungrateful. If he had not thought it would hurt her to refuse them, he would have begged off. He was trapped by that perception, however, and took them home.

His parents' hi-fi dominated a room, but it had just recently made the crossing. To fill in, they had bought a portable record player that became his by neglect and default. The songs from the box were old, no longer played on the radio, but he controlled them and that was new.

Later, there were borrowed records, which he played until he worried they were damaged. They had been lent by the family's Danish friend, Niels Adler, who judged he needed them.

"Detachment is too much to ask of the very young," said Mr. Adler as he flicked through the rows of albums on his shelves. "But humor is a beginning. If it grows into irony, one has started to make progress."

He wanted Holzli to listen to Tom Lehrer and to Flanders and Swann, and Holzli found this easy.

His wife, Fiona, was Scottish and from her one got information about the Adlers themselves. Mr. Adler discouraged the personal.

"What do you know about Denmark?" he asked Holzli once, and this was as near as he let the boy approach to anything bearing on himself.

"Well," Holzli replied, hesitating, not sure his answer would be seen for a joke. "I know the pastries."

This was not strictly true. He had no idea what the pastries were like.

"In Denmark, we call those Viennese pastries. Good, though—you now know all anyone needs to know about Denmark. *Chess*—that's what you need to learn about."

They did play chess, whenever the Lloyds had reason to go to the larger town. Holzli never won.

Late in February, they stopped by the Adlers when they came into town for *Karneval,* the Mardi Gras festival. That was as far as Holzli's parents got. While they stayed to drink beer in the apartment, he went out on his own to see what might be seen.

The streets were roiled by a population in costume with floats and signs and music. Holzli himself had a costume he had, in the end, not worn. It was a cowboy outfit, chosen for its anonymity—it prevailed with boys his age—and for its accoutrements: revolvers were sold, fake but armed with brass caps like miniature blanks which were loaded into the cylinder like real bullets and discharged by a hammer with a firing-pin. These were popular independently of costume or age, but only really fitted with the Western gear. Still, Holzli lost his nerve and could not bring himself to wear any of it in public.

How much allure the Western theme had intrinsically and how much was reflected from the Winnetou movies, he could not tell. Like everyone else in the school, he collected the cards showing scenes from the films. Just in the past week, he had finally seen the first installment in the series, though not in a theater. A boy from school, the son of a wealthy Italian-Swiss family that lived across the valley, invited him over to watch his own eight-millimeter copy.

The Indians were too Italian, the German presence too gratuitous, and the country little like Roswell, New Mexico, where he had been once. But it was no worse, for all of that, than any Hollywood product he had seen. The scenes with the buffalo were impressive; he wondered where they had gotten the herd. The movie starred someone he remembered as Tarzan, but that was his problem, not the film's. If, in the end, he was left cold, it was, he thought, because he was not European enough to love the West enough.

Whatever the source of the West's appeal, none of it passed to Holzli. He disappointed as an American. On a map, he had shown his classmates where he came from, and they noted how distant from the West all his places were. He also—not from malice but too casually—was cruelly literal when asked to translate "cowboy." He could not now be seen in dress he was known not to merit and to which he was held unsympathetic. Even in the town he might be recognized.

In the celebration but not of it, he was losing interest even before the first suggestion of migraine came to him. It was not a headache—it was a state, the taste of which carried with it a despair as bad, almost, as the full assault would be.

He realized, as soon as he decided to return, that he had not paid attention when he left the apartment. There were no sights or places he remembered being near the building. Were this a familiar part of the town, those associations would have come without thinking, but he had spent little time in this neighborhood when he lived in the Hotel

Bahnhof. Walking, waiting for inspiration, did not help. The exercise only made his head throb behind the eye and sickened his stomach.

He circled through the streets he knew must hold the building, hoping with each circuit for something to obtrude, some clue he missed on each previous passage.

He had been through this before. A bus ride round about Taipei deprived him of all mooring while he waited for his bus stop to reveal itself. En route from Taiwan to California, they stopped in Honolulu for three days, staying in the vacation apartment of one of his father's colleagues. Coming back from Waikiki, where he had burned himself red during a surfing lesson, Holzli found he had no inkling what the building looked like from outside. He walked till his skin bubbled.

Chance rescued him both times, and he knew this too would end, but he felt doomed always to lose his origins. He was not convinced that his attention was entirely at fault—his beginnings, he suspected, would always change beyond recognition as soon as his back was turned.

The migraine was pressing on him and all the festivity turned strained and hollow and mocking, a collective sarcasm directed at him. The bright colors hurt his eyes and were meant to. He saw a side street, tiny enough that no part of the crowd spilled over into it, and ran down it. A third through the block, he vomited into a hedge and looked around immediately, expecting a Swiss scolding.

There, above him, was the apartment building. He was functional once more, as he always was at this point—the migraines built toward this then ebbed away. A walkway he knew led him to the ground floor entrance.

Up two flights of stairs, the door opened at once to his knock.

"Are you ready to go?" his father asked and picked up his hat without waiting for an answer.

"Yep. I've seen everything, I think."

Mr. Adler helped Holzli's mother with her coat and said, "I've been trying to talk your parents into visiting Einsiedeln."

The boy looked to his father, who said, "It's an abbey in Schwyz," and waved him back to the Dane.

"A Benedictine abbey," said Mr. Adler. "You'd be visiting the big abbey church, which is worth looking at in itself, but it's what's inside that's supposed to be the goal of the pilgrimage.

"It's a black Madonna."

He watched for some response in Holzli and got none. "Black Madonnas are an interesting phenomenon. I've seen about thirty throughout Europe and I've read that there are about two hundred. They're all objects of pilgrimage."

"Mr. Adler was saying he thinks they're pre-Christian," Holzli's mother put in.

"The originals were, I think," Mr. Adler said. "The sites seem to have pagan associations and the black color itself is telling. It's the color of rich soil, of fertility.

"They take great care to explain away the black. They're sensitive about it—if they didn't make a point of it, it wouldn't get as much attention. Usually, the story is that the statue has been darkened by soot from candles and lamps.

"You'll see that the one at Einsiedeln is painted black, and that's a twisty little tale. By the way, do you want anything to drink before you go?"

"He'd better not," Holzli's father answered. "We need to get back before it's too late."

"Well, Saint Meinrad supposedly brought the original statue with him when he set up his hermitage where the Lady Chapel is now inside the big church. That one was lost in a fire, and the present statue was carved in the 1400's.

"Napoleon's people tried to stop the pilgrimages. They plundered the place and burned the chapel, and they thought they packed the Lady off to Paris. They had an imposter, though—the real one had been spirited away by her devotees and had a series of adventures before being returned. By then, she needed a professional restoration job.

"This is where the canonical story kicked in. The restorer claimed to find that Mary's skin color came from smoke, and he painted her Caucasian. There were too many complaints, however, and she had to be renegrified as she is now.

"Why can't that be the true story?" Holzli asked. "Wouldn't candles really do that?"

"Perhaps. But why does it only affect Madonnas this way? And why doesn't anything around them turn black? And why does it only affect their faces and hands?"

Holzli's father moved toward the door. "Apparently we need to see this place since we're in Switzerland," he said. "I guess we should go—I've heard the frescoes are impressive if a bit...overdone."

Outside, the day was dimming and a chill was coming on, but Holzli thought it might be noisier than it had been during his wanderings. His father slid the car slowly between revelers and out of the town. He fumbled with the radio and they were nearly trampled by Nancy Sinatra before he managed to turn it off again.

CHAPTER 13

There were two stops where Konrad could reasonably get off, and Holzli chose the closest. He waited by a square stone pillar at the corner of a wrought-iron fence where Konrad would not be likely to see him until too late.

It worked, and as soon the tram doors hissed shut, he stepped into the German's sight. Konrad looked at him and walked on without a greeting or change of expression.

Holzli matched his pace but could not draw his eye. It had not been light long, and the air had not had time to warm. Holzli's face was numb, and he had to walk with his hands pushed deep into his pockets. Konrad quickened his stride almost to running, free to swing his gloved hands in wide arcs.

"I need to talk to you," Holzli said, forced to speech finally as they neared the Seefeldquai. The other gave no response.

"I've heard Mark's whole story. I don't know what to make of it now. It's got too many details. I'd decided it was all his regular crap, but it sounds too real. I don't know that he's smart enough to make something like this up."

Konrad stopped and turned. "But those are not the only possibilities. He can be getting it all from somewhere else."

"What are you talking about?"

"He can be getting it all from books. Really, all he is telling us could be from some novel. Or, maybe, he's just getting things from a history book and throwing in this dream girl."

"So there's no way to know."

They had started walking again, but slowly—there was time before school, and they would have nothing to do if they arrived early but sit in the stairwell.

"Do you see him with books?" Konrad asked.

"Just that flying saucer thing. I just don't remember anything else he's ever read. He sure doesn't do the assigned readings."

The first floor of the mansion was warmer than the street by a hair, but only offices were there. Classrooms were on the higher floors, the levels of the classes ascending with height. The temperature in the common, central spaces rose, too. Circling round the third floor on their way to the fourth, the two boys passed the room that packaged the library.

It was closed this early, but Holzli noticed its broad, brown door as a matter of course; he had fond feelings for it. He had been gratified by how good a collection it held. It was one of the few pleasant discoveries of his early days in the school.

The stock was weighted oddly, probably by the accidents of donation. Holzli had let the oddities shape his reading: for the last two months he had read mostly H. Rider Haggard, Egyptian history, and the Biggles books. Someone had followed James Bigglesworth through both wars and beyond, and somehow the school now owned it all.

"You spend all your time in the library," Konrad stated self-certainly.

"I do *not*."

"What kind of history books does it have?"

"All sorts. They have a couple shelves for history."

"Swiss history?"

"That I don't know."

They had been climbing fast enough to wind them both. Konrad did not speak for a moment, gathering his breath, and Holzli had time to understand. "You want to check out Mark's story—see if it fits with anything."

"*Ja.* Let's come back down at lunch. We should at least be able to pin it down to a time. Or not. Either would be good."

They hurried down when Algebra ended too many minutes into the lunch hour, afraid that Frau Geiger would leave to eat before they could catch her. She was not a librarian full time—the library was small for that—but she had her desk in there and looked after the books while she did the school's clerical work.

They reached the door as she was coming out and, without thinking, took positions to block her way.

"Am I being kidnapped?" she asked.

"Oh, no," said Konrad, embarrassed to realize what they had done, and both boys stepped back as if she had pulled a knife.

"We have a question about something," Holzli said at once to reinforce their harmlessness. He did not have the question yet, though, and Frau Geiger looked her own question at him, waiting for him to go on.

Konrad took another turn: "We need to find a book."

"Or books," added Holzli.

"About Swiss history," said Konrad, after a pause.

"Oh, well, we have many books about that." Frau Geiger withdrew into the library and jerked her hand at shelves to her right. "This whole row three down."

"But just one time in history," Holzli expanded.

"And we do not know what it is," his friend contributed.

Holzli knew, from direct experience, that the woman's patience did not bear strain. Her face, even now, was growing stony. What to say?

"Do you know what a Baptizer is?" he asked.

"A baptizer?" Her expression continued to set.

"A *Taüfer,* maybe," suggested Konrad.

"Do you mean liked a *Wiedertaüfer*? A Rebaptizer? The heretics?" She put her thumb and forefinger to her brow. "That's not what you call them in English."

She stared at Holzli. "What do you call them?"

He could not tell if this was a real question. He shrugged.

"An *Anabaptist,*" she dragged up at last. "That is the word."

Holzli nodded, trying to keep her happy.

She went to the corner where the novels were kept. "This will do you better than a history book." She ran her finger over the spines, poking some volumes back into alignment or hooking them forward. "Where is it?"

She turned and glared at them, again leaving them unsure whether to attempt an answer.

"I cannot find it." It sounded like an accusation.

"What is it?" Konrad asked with forced innocence.

"It is a story by Gottfried Keller, the great Zurich writer. It is *Ursula*. You need to read him anyway.

"I will look at the cards but I do not remember anyone checking it out."

The cards would not mean much, Holzli knew. The library was often unattended, and students sometimes just borrowed the books without signing the cards.

"Nothing here," Frau Geiger announced. "Well, let us see what is in the history section."

She moved to that shelf and scanned it. "Ah! Here is what you want!" Prying out a slender volume, she pulled its cover off and said something sibilant under her breath.

Nesting the bare slab of pages within the cover again, she handed the thing to Holzli. "Here. Do not let it come apart. Sign the card."

The cover was grey cardboard with a typed sticker that read: *The Birth of Swiss Anabaptism*. Someone had handwritten "Author: Philip S. Corbett" in pencil. The leaves were yellow around the edges and some were loose.

While Holzli signed, Frau Geiger yanked the drawers of her desk open until she found a large rubber band. "Put this around it," she commanded. "It has lost its real cover and it will not stay together by itself."

She held the rubber band out but snatched it away as he was about to take it. "Give me the book," she said.

Puzzled, he handed it back. She examined the sticker on the front and drew out a drawer in the big card catalogue. Flicking through the contents with a scarlet fingernail, she grunted. "Good. We have another copy somewhere."

She stretched the rubber band around the book and tried to fit the result back onto its shelf but gave up. "No other there," she muttered almost inaudibly.

Another visit to the tray of signed cards on her desk yielded nothing either. "I suppose you must take this," she told the boys, passing the rebound copy over again. "This would never happen in a Swiss school."

"Who's going to look through this?" Holzli asked Konrad as they climbed back up to get their lunches.

"You are. I still have not written my *Macbeth* essay. You will have to report back to me."

They moved aside to avoid Margaret Owens, who was coming down the stairs singing "Distant Shores" to herself in what she imagined was an English accent. She sneered at them and looked away.

"I, for one," Konrad resumed, "would like to know who has those books. That is very strange."

"If Mark has them, it doesn't show anything—we wouldn't know how long he's had them. Just like him not to sign them out."

"But who else would read about these *Wiedertaüfer*? We did not learn anything about them in History. They must be some sort of Reformers, but all Mr. Austin talked about was Zwingli and Luther."

Holzli himself had an essay on the Benelux countries to finish before the last class of the day. He had the library book out to read when he boarded the tram after school, but an old lady wanted his seat and he had to stand all the way to the Hauptbahnhof. At the station, he rushed to see if he could catch the express, pausing only to buy a package of Läkerol from the tiny, tin vending machine near the side doors. That robbed him of enough time, however, that he was left for the local. He did not really care—it gave him leisure, finally, to unbundle the book.

CHAPTER 14

Holzli was free for the Mardi Gras *Karneval* because the village school took that day off. The day before had been a holiday itself, really, since the school had its own *Fasnacht* celebration then. The morning had been classes but, at noon, they were released to go to the gym where booths were set up with food and games. The central attraction was a puppet show in Schwyzerdütsch so heavy it sounded as if someone had set out deliberately to destroy a manual transmission.

Lent would have meant little in their household had Holzli not insisted that their meals conform. This battle had been won years before when he started refusing to eat what was served when it violated fast or abstinence. Whatever else his parents ate he did not care; that was on their consciences—his was clear.

He kept expecting the trip to Einsiedeln, thinking that had been settled on at the Adlers, but nothing more was said of it for weeks.

"Here now is what you *don't* want religions doing," his father said, one evening, rattling his *Herald Tribune* after turning pages to follow an article. "The Vietnamese are having to bring in troops to keep the Buddhists under control. Enthusiasm is not what we need."

The paper went to his lap. "Interesting word, that, though. Taken literally. That reminds me—I was thinking we'd go to Einsiedeln at Easter, but Niels says the crowds will be too much. We should drive down this Sunday if we're going to go."

They started late and went through Zürich, then south a few kilometers into Schwyz. They were in the folds of the Alps' skirts, and the valleys through which they drove rose higher and more sharply than anything near the village. Holzli did not trust that the cows on the slopes could keep their balances—he kept expecting one to topple and roll at the car like a boulder, picking up speed as it came, spinning in bands of brown and white.

The town they reached flowed down from the abbey on another steep hill side. When they finished the climb up the cobblestone street, the abbey church confronted them across an immense, tilted square to its front. Between were a polygonal fountain with spouts on each face and two curved horns of booths like the wings of an enveloping army. Nothing, though, challenged the eye as the church itself did, a fortress with two towers that could pass for the frame of a sally port in cyclopean walls.

People were revolving around the fountain, drinking from the spouts in turn. "I want to drink," Holzli told his mother. "Read the sign and see why we're doing it."

"It says the water flows under the Madonna's altar."

"But what does it do?" he asked, wiping his mouth with the back of his hand.

"Apparently it doesn't do anything. Or they would say something about it. Nobody told you to drink it."

They climbed again to reach the main doors, and entered, the parents with the momentum that had carried them up over the mossy stones, Holzli more diffident, concerned to locate holy water with real potency.

He stayed with his parents as they toured the series of altars that lined the walls until he could no longer take his father's snideness and volume. On his own, he found a formidable organ, high in the air, ornate far beyond function, with little angels on the pipes that would set his father near to cackling when he came on it.

The altar to a St. Mauritius kept him for a time. Its honoree was flanked by St. Michael and St. George, both of whom, as warriors, repelled and drew him. He knelt for a time.

They met up again at the chapel of the Madonna herself, back by the entrance. *"Nigra Sum, Sed Formosa,"* his father read aloud from a booklet. "Does she look like Taiwan?" he asked his son.

The crowned and robed and slippered Lady held a crowned, robed child. The back of her recess was a radiating aureole. Right before the chapel, people kneeled, one a boy a little older than Holzli.

"Well, the chapel and the statue aren't quite a match, but that's to be expected." His father's voice made Holzli jump, lancing deep into his thoughts without warning and booming by contrast with the scene. "The vestments are a nasty touch, though. Apparently they change them with the liturgical season. Almost Mexican in vulgarity."

The kneeling boy opened his eyes and turned, contempt twisting his face, too fierce and elemental to be moderated. It was not directed at Holzli's father, though—who would not have seen it regardless—but at Holzli, who had thought to kneel himself but now only wanted to leave, quickly, silently, inconspicuously.

They left, mercifully, to look at the stables where the monks kept horses. Coming out and continuing around the complex, they found two stations of the cross on a path that then took off up the hill. They were still nowhere near the top.

"Can we do the rest of them?" Holzli asked.

"No," his father said. "We can go on a bit, but we don't feel like doing any more climbing."

Another station stood in a grove protruding off the path into a slanted meadow. A little ahead was the fourth station, mobbed by horses, some with their heads stretched through the fence into the enclosure.

"The Fourth Station," intoned his mother. "'Jesus Has Sugar in His Pockets.'"

The horses did not move away when they got there but were not interested in them, either. Nothing was there that should have attracted horses.

"There's an adoration in the undercroft and some sort of ceremony at the chapel, later, but that's it for the abbey," Holzli's father gathered from the booklet. "If we're going to eat and get home before too late, we'd better mosey back to town and see what's available."

Nothing much was, it being Sunday. The couple places open nearby, run by Italians to accommodate the pilgrims and tourists, were overfull. Inertia kept the three from leaving immediately. They continued further down through the town, peering into shop windows.

"Who are you supposed to be?" Holzli's father asked a figurine standing on a platform in one window, clasping a book to its breast with one arm and a massive sword, its point to the ground, with the other, facing down a wooden bear on skis. He squinted at the first figure's base. "Ulrich Zwingli. Oh, this is that statue by the Grossmünster—without the bear. Why do they have this here? This should be hostile territory."

His wife now carried the guide booklet and she opened it to the back. "I remember something about that. Wasn't he...here it is. There's a section on general history. Let's see— Paracelsus was born near here and...'Huldrych Zwingli was a parish priest in Einsiedeln after transferring from Glarus. Secular rather than Benedictine, Zwingli was critical of the pilgrimage and the 'superstition' it entailed—as might be expected of a father of the Reformation. He left to be a People's Pastor in Zürich in 1519, and the rest is history.'"

Riding through the silence of Zürich on the way home, Holzli could hear a bell toll somewhere far off.

"That might be the Grossmünster," his mother commented, a strange, distracted expression on her face. "Probably not, though, I guess, at this distance."

It sounded to Holzli like the bell at the start of *Lights Out*, the one that measured the narrator's "It...is...later... than...you...think." He looked to the south where they had been, but it was already too dark to see anything but the vague bulk of the mountains edging the sky.

CHAPTER 15

"Okay, here's the report..." Holzli started, but Konrad held up his palm to stop him.

"I, too, have a report to make."

"On what?"

"I found both books on Mark—the Ursula one and the good copy of your book. He had them in his bag."

"How did you know they were there?"

"I merely assumed they were there. I caught him yesterday after school and took his bag and opened it."

"What did he do?"

"Nothing until I found the books. It all happened too fast for him."

This morning was colder than yesterday's. Rain drizzled. Holzli loved rain; it gave a background to the day—set it in a context—that broke routine even if nothing else changed.

They would be kept inside all day, but that was little enough to pay. All during classes, he would have a channel to freedom: the sight of dark clouds through the windows, rolling high over borders, unbound by gravity, unburdened by expectations, would take him away from this place.

It brought sorrow, too, which he savored. Something connected with the absence of borders and constraint.

Finitude was lacking—forms were not natural or lasting. Things perished because their identities were not fixed. Loss was the world's very essence. That sometimes saddened him so exquisitely his fingers tingled, but, mostly, he just nestled in a warm, heavy melancholy.

"He claims he only borrowed the books after his experiences. But who can tell?"

"Did you read them?"

"I kept the *Ursula* and read it last night—it was so short. The Corbett book was your job. I left Mark his copy."

"Well, I looked through the Corbett book. It's long."

"Was it funny? These Anabaptists were just clowns if Keller is fair. His book is very comical."

"I didn't find anything like that."

Holzli's trench coat was up to rain this light, but he had no umbrella or hat, and his hands froze whenever they left his pockets. He thought of a warmer rain over the village early that summer that had left a rainbow in the sun. One end had been lost in the mist of the river valley, and the other came down in the hills opposite. While he dressed to climb up there, it disappeared. He went anyway—the bow had left a charm on the landscape, and the green meadows over there were changed. They promised something beyond themselves.

"Then, deliver your report," Konrad demanded.

The American ordered his information. This was like an essay exam. "I'll only give the history stuff. It goes along with Mark's story..."

"It may be the *source* of Mark's story."

"I know, I know." Konrad had little techniques for usurping superiority. "The other things are interesting, too, but here's the history part.

"So, you have Zwingli coming to Zürich at the end of 1518. You know some of this stuff from Mr. Austin. Zwingli's still Catholic, and the city council makes him a priest at the big church, the Grossmünster. He still gets money—some sort of pension—from Rome for a couple years.

"He starts moving away from the Church, though, pretty quickly. He wants people to stop hiring out as mercenaries to the Pope and his enemies, and he wants all sorts of

Protestant things like doing away with the Mass. He's able to talk the council into going along with most of it."

"Wait. How does the council make him a priest to begin with?"

"Okay, a pastor, not a priest. But I don't know how it does that. It's weird. The city seems to have been in charge of that sort of thing even in Catholic times. It went way back. But, anyway, everyone's used to the local government making these decisions, so if Zwingli can talk them into doing things, everybody goes along."

They had dawdled as much as they could, but, nevertheless, they now stood on the walk before the school. Others were arriving and rushing in, splashing their way through puddles to beat the bell.

"Lunch," pronounced Konrad, and Holzli grunted assent. He was just starting to build momentum, and it was jarring to stop like this, but they would be late for first-hour French if they did not hurry up the stairs.

Lunch for Holzli consistently featured yogurt since he discovered it. In the States, it was an occult pleasure, reserved for health nuts. He had never seen it before chancing on it in a shop and buying some from curiosity. It was useful as a lubricant when boluses of sandwich—smuggled peanut butter on the leathery local bread—threatened to choke him.

He escaped this peril one last time right as Konrad finished his own meal, sausages and cheese and a *Bürli* roll. *"Na,* then," the latter said, "Zwingli begins to change things."

"Yeah. He turns into the most important religious person in the city. It looks like he had a pretty easy time of it—the book calls him a 'master politician.' There are some people who want to go slow—there's a guy named Jacob Grebel who has a lot of power and gets in the way—but some people want even faster changes. Jacob Grebel's son, whose name is—get ready—Conrad..."

"That is a very common name."

"Whatever. Anyway, this Conrad knows how to spell his own name right, with a 'C.' He's a big radical. So, like, there's some strange thing going on with his father."

His listener just shrugged, without expression, so Holzli continued, "At first, Zwingli and Conrad are big buddies. They agree on all kinds of new ideas like not baptizing babies or that Christians shouldn't use violence. As time goes on, though, Zwingli stops pushing for the new ideas, and Conrad and his other friends turn against him. They start turning into the Anabaptists.

"Other things are going on at the same time. Some people are telling farmers that they shouldn't be forced to pay tithes and taxes to the Church and to the nobles. A monastery gets sacked. Not much else happens locally, but, later, there are uprisings in Germany and other places that are pretty violent. People connected with the Anabaptists are involved, but Conrad and his group talk against violence from the beginning."

It was hard to put it all in order and, already, he was forgetting things. "Oh, wait, this is important. This Felix Manz that Mark talks about—he's part of this bunch that hangs around with Conrad and Zwingli at the beginning. They have a Greek study group and read and discuss Plato. Manz is the son of a priest at the Grossmünster, so he has connections.

"It's through these guys, by the way, that Zwingli gets taken seriously. Manz isn't nearly as valuable as the Grebels—they're some sort of nobility and Jacob was the Mayor at one point.

"So, anyway, Zwingli starts to back down on a lot of things—too many for Conrad and not enough for Jacob. Pretty soon, though, he becomes more powerful than them and doesn't need them. And Conrad and his friends turn more and more...extreme. It leads to some debates in the City Hall. I couldn't keep track of all of them, but Zwingli wins them all. Finally, he gets laws passed against the Anabaptists, mostly threatening anyone who gets rebaptized or doesn't baptize his kids.

"Oh, and he manages to set up a secret council to plan war against the Catholic cantons".

"I do not understand all this concern with baptism."

"I don't either. It doesn't seem very interesting. But I haven't read very much of the book. The other things the

Anabaptists complain about—violence and government—are more interesting"

Konrad started to laugh, but a particle of food had escaped him and now flew from his mouth. He clamped his lips tightly together, embarrassed, and placed his foot over the missile, which had landed just before him. He swallowed, for security, and said, "They were against government?"

"I can't tell. I don't think so. It seems confused. They were against taking part in it, anyway, because it meant making people behave by threatening them with violence. That's what Zwingli thought, too, at first, but he changed his mind big time."

"Therefore, that is why he was against the mercenaries."

"Not just because of that, I think. He didn't change his mind on the mercenaries. They weren't happy with him, though—I forgot to mention that. Some of them go to his house one night and break all his windows and try to get him to come out and fight. He doesn't. They yell that he's a seducer from Glarus and a thief. Someone rides a horse into the Grossmünster and calls him a thief, too, and a heretic, but I think that guy may just be Catholic.

"Then, in 1525, things start heating up. The city council passes a law that all babies have to be baptized."

"I thought they already did that."

"This is when they do it."

"Well, put things in better order."

"Look, I didn't have much time to spend on this. You only read that novel and you say it's pretty short."

"Here, you can read it if you want." Konrad reached around behind himself for the books he had bound with a rubber strap. He worked out a thin, red book and threw it in Holzli's lap.

"Do you want the one I'm reading?" Holzli asked.

"No. I am only saying that, if you are going to report on it, do not confuse things."

"I'm just trying to find the important stuff. What Mark might have used. I'm not trying to do a book report."

"You are angry?" Konrad was careful to smirk, but it did not cover his surprise.

"No," said Holzli. But now that the other mentioned it, he knew he was.

Something quivered in his throat, although he kept most of it out of his voice. "They also ordered Grebel and Manz and Blaurock not to meet or to talk about religion in public."

He kept his voice flat and locked his eyes on Konrad's. "I know I haven't mentioned Blaurock. I'm mentioning him now."

Konrad took the warning and Holzli went on, "He's Mark's Blue Coat, obviously. He comes to town and hooks up with Grebel. That's not his name—everyone calls him that because it's what he wears. I forget his real name. Georg something. He's another priest gone bad.

"He and the rest of Grebel's people decide they're going to make a clean break with everybody else by baptizing each other. Blaurock gets Conrad to baptize him and then he baptizes everyone else. This all takes place in Manz' house somewhere around the Grossmünster.

"After that, things fit Mark's story pretty well. There's a meeting at Rüdi Thomann's house in Zollikon a few days later with more baptisms, then every one starts baptizing, especially around Zollikon, then you have a bunch of laws and arrests and escapes and executions. Conrad leaves town after an escape and dies of the plague before he can ever come back. There's a lot of it going around right then. A few months later, Zwingli has Jacob Grebel tortured and killed. Corbett thinks it's just revenge, since there weren't any good reasons for it—Jacob was more against the Anabaptists than Zwingli was and Conrad had been dead so long.

"After that, Anabaptism spreads over Europe. They're hunted down and tortured and killed everywhere—both Protestants and Catholics agree that it's a good idea. Usually, they burn them if they catch them.

"Finally, the Anabaptists turn into Mennonites and Amish and move to Pennsylvania. I didn't have any idea that's who I was reading about! "

This had intrigued the boy most in the whole account, and his excitement had been keen enough to warrant suppressing. The residue of his anger at Konrad departed now in the presence of this fact.

"We used to drive out there sometimes, on the other side of Philadelphia, when we lived in Jersey. My mother liked to look for furniture and quilts there."

Konrad could not be warmed to any degree of enthusiasm. He said, "So Mark can have gotten everything from this book."

"I suppose."

"Do we know where in Zollikon this Thomann house is?"

"Well, yeah. The book gives an address on Gstadstrasse. But Mark told us that anyway. It's that house near where he lives. With a plaque on it! That's what he keeps saying!"

"So the plaque probably tells what happened there, and Mark has seen it every day for who knows how long."

"And after a few months, even Mark would wonder what it said and manage to translate it."

They sat wordless until Konrad had to speak the obvious. "We must go to that house, see that plaque. It would be nice to meet Mark there, but that would be too hard. But he needs to be shown that we know all."

"When?"

"This afternoon. Or, maybe we can wait until a day when we are certain he is walking home and take the train and beat him there."

"I would want to take the train anyway. I don't have much time in the afternoons before I have to be home. And it can't be today, and I have to know which day, beforehand, because I need to make up a story for my parents for why I'm late."

"Monday, then, whether he walks or not."

"He always walks."

CHAPTER 16

In April, Sandoz Pharmaceuticals, in Basel, announced that it would stop the sale of LSD. Back in Washington, Senator Edward Kennedy was pushing to have it outlawed altogether. Holzli followed things as well as he could through a derivative interest: he knew that the drug had been developed as a remedy for migraines. It was related to cafergot, which had failed for him in Virginia. He hoped, someday, to come across some testimony—some side-comment, dropped in passing—that LSD served its intended purpose.

He was willing to brave the side-effects. There was little promise else. Aspirin was beneath contempt; one might as well swallow chalk. He had not been able to keep codeine down. No stronger measures had been offered him.

"A bit of a disappointment, I understand," his father had remarked once when the subject came up on the armed forces radio news.

"It didn't do *anything* for headaches?" Holzli had asked.

"Headaches? What are you talking about?" his father responded, wrinkling with annoyance, and would say nothing more.

It did not matter. It did not look now as though he would ever encounter the drug. Then, again, he knew it and other drugs, already forbidden, were more and more popular Stateside. As far as he was aware, they had no presence in the village, which grudgingly admitted the twentieth century at all, but they were in the music he listened to, riding electromagnetic waves across oceans and frontiers. The pirate stations and the American military delivered them to his home.

"Rainy Day Women" was the most peculiar and intriguing delivery. It became only marginally more accessible after a Canadian boy at the church in Zürich explained what "stoned" now meant.

That was the one Sunday they stayed for the social hour after the service. Allen Dulles was attending that day. The adults and the people Holzli's age went to different sides of the vast social hall as if gravitating to opposite poles. The children in the international school fell easily into talk, but it took him time to identify another outdweller. They shared only radio and the Swiss school system. The other's school did not sound as bad as his.

He looked over from time to time to see his parents in a group around an older man who looked like his father with a pipe and thicker, white hair.

"He's John Foster Dulles' brother, you know," his father told him on the road home. "The old Secretary of State."

Holzli grunted. He supposed he was disappointed they had not gotten the more prominent brother but he was pondering the Canadian boy's hair. It was long, like a rock musician's, and he could not imagine showing up at his own village school like that.

He had enough trouble finding the boundaries of convention. His worst misstep had been a dickey his mother had found somewhere. It passed as a turtleneck—risky in itself, perhaps, but imaginable—until he had to change for gym. He would not wear it again.

"Pretty long hair on that boy you were talking to," his father said as they left the fringes of the city and entered the fields. There were no houses here—there were no farmsteads. Farmers lived in towns and commuted to their work. Holzli saw a cat through the rear car window, a grey tabby, positioned in one field to guard a rodent hole.

"I couldn't tell whether he was a girl or a boy for a minute," his father continued.

The man was obsessed with hair. Holzli had not succeeded in having his cut like Sean Connery's because even that was too long in the back. His father knew this from a pictorial of the actor in an Italian magazine Holzli bought. It featured Connery's hair especially, for a reason the father made certain the son noticed: in close-ups, one could see a sort of mesh under the hair at the front.

"I don't know what the U.S. is coming to. I'm glad we got you out before this started. Maybe they can have things cleaned up before you move back."

The road did not cling to the Limmat, but it was tethered to it. The car left and met the river all the way to the big town south of the village. The river below their house, though, did not flow into or out of this valley; it was born of its own three springs and emptied into the Rhine. The way home cut across high ground to reach their own valley, then dropped steeply to the floor. Holzli did not like the descent in the dark.

"This country may be too small and too obsessed with this neutrality claptrap, but it knows how to order its citizenry. It doesn't put up with conscientious objector types, for one thing. Straight to prison. These people still have shared values." He looked back at Holzli with a tight-lipped smile. "The girls in your school even understand modesty."

Holzli supposed this had something to do with the girls' braids and full dresses and aprons. These all provided a paradoxical allure, as far as he was concerned, but he had learned his father's mind worked differently from his. Their perceptions had never quite coincided on anything he could remember.

He knew his father did not understand the Swiss. They were too consistent in their character, if not, deep down, unitary. He could not have explained this—he did not fully grasp it—but he sensed it about them. He sensed nothing like it in his parent, who was not even coherent on the surface.

Herr Lehrer Ehrlich had spent a good part of a morning earlier that week discoursing on the senselessness of the

Gemini space program, which had just done a docking experiment. The teacher professed to lack the mistiest inkling of comprehension why anyone would go into space. It violated limits for the sake of violation. It left men drifting in the middle of nothing.

But, Americans did that sort of thing. Herr Ehrlich carefully did not look at Holzli. It was like their war in Vietnam, transgression in the strictest sense and to no other end. Communism, of course, was bad, too, but was moved by the same spirit.

You could see this working itself out in Hollywood. There was nothing wrong with movies. They used to be good. They had changed, however, and changed to change. And now they had no form—they were entirely the lowest things: guns and women. Herr Ehrlich shrugged his shoulders and returned to the arithmetic on the board.

There was no *Kino* in the village. Holzli had to go to the big town or Zürich to see movies. There were few he was old enough to see, and those allowed him were old. The Cinema Manzo discovered that silent comedies from the teens and twenties drew big. For a time, he had a regular place there— the same seat among the same old men—and watched Fatty Arbuckle and Laurel and Hardy until they were too familiar.

Other theaters had more recent things. He sat in the flickering darkness and listened to the audience watch the films.

"Autos im Kino?" a voice, whispery with wonder, asked some unseen other behind Holzli when a drive-in theater appeared on the screen. He realized how much of these people's picture of America was given inadvertently by filmmakers on their way to other things. How real the watchers took these details for, he could not tell. Even for him, they were scenes from a land of entertainment, not likely to be part of his experience.

The Lloyds themselves were diversions. When they sat out behind their house, dining or lounging on the small flat area they had at the bottom of a grassy slope, tour buses would stop and empty onto the road above. The tour guides would point them out and explain them.

These were not locals, but something of the same could happen Sundays when the village took its walk. The promenaders headed for high ground, and that brought some to the road overlooking the house.

The Lloyds started to join in the custom—to seize that ground for themselves. Each Sunday, when they returned from Zürich, they kept their dress clothes on and climbed the slope. Not much more was expected of them than to walk a couple of hours, wherever they pleased, and contemplate views and say *"grüezi mitenand"* to other groups they met. It was enough to keep them from being one of the views.

Holzli's weekly migraine sometimes came on before the family returned down the slope, but that scarcely mattered. All places were the same once the headache started.

CHAPTER 17

Ursula was short enough that he had almost finished it by the time the bus released him in the village. He had thought, briefly, that he would be able to read on the tram. An old woman demanded his seat, and he responded, *"Nei, du hässliches altes Weibchen!"* This refusal and insult, premeditated and prepared, took all his assertiveness. He had none left actually to look up and observe the effect. She left, however, and that was satisfactory. He had relaxed and popped the latches on his attaché case.

The woman returned with the conductor, and Holzli stood for the rest of the journey. In the train, he tried for the book again. The case was cheap and old; the brass latches stuck and had to be prised open sometimes with a coin.

A one-*Frank* piece would do. This was the size and color of a quarter and worth about as much. Swiss money was convenient in that way: the two-*Frank* piece looked like a fifty-cent piece and was near it in value; the fifty-*Rappen* piece, a half-*Frank,* was worth about a dime and resembled one; the twenty-*Rappen* piece was the twin of a nickel; the five-*Rappen* piece was small and copper. His father had said, though, that someday currencies might float—change relative to each other. That would spoil the marvelous correspondence.

He missed the backpack. It lay in his closet, now, defaced but whole and usable. The incident on the train platform had been more a pretext for abandoning it than a functional reason. The pack had made him vulnerable to the chemical people. He had stood by it, but only until he could desert it in good conscience. The case was cardboard covered in leather-like green. It smelled like old newspapers. The pack had smelled of cowhide.

It had been day when he entered the train, but that did not last out the trip any more. When lights came on in the buildings he passed, he set the book down on his knee and rested his forehead against the glass. It burned like ice.

Keller's Anabaptists were nothing like Corbett's. Holzli did not know how to take the book. It was tempting to see it as the other side of the case—some thing to be matched against the other book at equal strength. There was a tone to it, however, he could not ignore. The writing had a smug, hateful smell that warned one off. It smelt of Herr Ehrlich.

And, then, despite all the writer could do, one could see the outlines of something beneath the prose that compelled. The disdain for weapons and the claim to a loyalty that aimed higher than human governments appealed to him, though comic characters articulated them.

"What is scripture?" he read. "An empty skin, a bag, if I do not blow the holy spirit into it! A dead cat, if I do not drive it to its feet with the breath of God! It is a tuneless pipe, a mute violin, if I do not play on it!" The speaker was a clownish megalomaniac, but something about that was right. "That vain grammarian and scholar may try his arts on this heap of dead letters. He might as usefully stir the sand of the desert—no living spring will start to flow."

"Here God is, there he is! He is everywhere!" preached another buffoon. "He is in the dust on this floor and in the salt of the sea water! He melts from the roof with the snow, we hear him drip, and he shines as dung in the lane! He frolics with the fish in the depths of the water and peers through the eye of the hawk, flying through the air. Why would wine be so pleasing, if he were not in it? How would bread satisfy, if he did not live in it? But he is also in us, and just as we only see ourselves if we have a mirror, so can we only see him who lives in us in the face of our neighbor and brother. Therefore, with diligence let us mirror ourselves in one another and be brothers that we may discover and reveal him, who has been in us from the very beginning!"

Holzli knew he was supposed to laugh, but he thought it was beautiful. Was it the echo of something real or was it only the author putting on the funniest voice he could imagine?

It was Friday. The international school took Saturdays off, so he could read and listen to the radio as far into the night as he wanted. Climbing the hill in the dark, he could not see the sky. Sometimes, the stars clustered in the thin air more thickly than he had ever seen in Asia or America. They sparkled in colors. Usually, as now, clouds hid them. The moon, too, was somewhere there behind the curtain—some folds of cloud glowed at their margins—but that was no help to him. He could make out the silhouette of the stone crucifix where the dirt road bent below his house. He could not read the inscription he knew was there: *Gott Schütze Land und Volk 1946.*

The wind rose and he felt drops. Rain carried no mood for him outside at night in black cold. There was no distance— one was too uncomfortable. He picked up his pace; he would have run, but so much of the road sloped thirty degrees or more.

Inside, late, when he was dry and warm and the house was quiet, he could take due delight in the sound of rain on the windows and the pavement around the house. It had fallen harder as the evening hours went by, and now it thrummed continuously. The radio was unthinkable; the sound would have defiled the night. He could barely read, so close to the edge of rapture.

He slept late and did not remember passing into sleep. His parents had left to shop in Zürich by the time he woke—he had told them at dinner he did not want to spend his Saturdays back in the city. Free, he finally finished the novel and then reread, slowly, the parts of Corbett he had scanned for Konrad.

The day was too cold to sit outside, but the sun shone without obstacle now that the clouds had poured themselves out. He sat at the dining table to read the rest of the history book. The table was next to the largest window in the house. It was not quite a picture window, but it gave a clear, broad view of the valley and the village and the hills beyond. From time to time, he looked up at the grassy prospect spreading and rolling in the sunlight. The farther meadows had the dreamlike, fantasy character they took on when the sun was bright enough and just the right height in the south. It had something to do with emptiness and distance.

Even the twilight was going by the time Holzli's parents burst in, rustling with bags. He left the books on the table to go down and help them.

"What have you been doing?" his father asked. "Something productive, I imagine."

Holzli did not know whether he was expected to rise to this sort of bait, but he never had. It could not repay the effort. He followed them back up the concrete stairs to the other floor. They unburdened themselves onto the table as a first step toward finding places for the purchases.

"What's this?" his father asked, picking up the books to clear a space.

"Things I'm reading."

"*Ursula,* by Gottfried Keller, and..." He squinted at the typing. "*The Birth of Swiss Anabaptism.* Keller I've heard of." He twisted toward his wife. "Don't we have a recording of something Delius did with one of his stories?"

Holzli's mother, unpacking and arranging, nodded, unhearing.

"But why are you reading this other thing?" Mr. Lloyd turned back to his son. "Anabaptists—weren't they some sort of peasant cult group?"

"They're the Amish and Mennonites. They started here, mostly around where you work and I go to school. That part of the city. And in Zollikon."

"I remember something about that. Finally made them leave. I never made the link with the modern groups." Mr. Lloyd put the books down on the counter that extended though a divider into the kitchen. He started taking things from bags. "But I do remember that the Anabaptists were driven out—and it makes sense now with the modern connection. From everywhere, like Gypsies. They contributed nothing, so no one wanted them around. Finally, of course, we ended up with them. The Canucks and us."

Through the window, Holzli could see that things were already shining with moonlight. Evening came earlier than needed—dusk started when the sun hit the hills above and behind them. As the year advanced and the sun retreated, those southern heights would rob him more and more of light.

"But they farm."

"For themselves and for the market. Not as part of the general polity." He was pulling out his lecture words. "They have no real loyalties."

Holzli did not often bother to disagree with his father, but this seemed a target too easy to let by. "They're loyal to their religion. And each other."

"But!" His father thrust a triumphant finger at him. "Their religion and their groups have no loyalty to the greater whole. They have no role—no identity—in the greater scheme of things. They might as well not exist except for shoofly pie and bad examples."

"Bad examples?"

"The Amish try to keep their kids out of public schools. And they've managed to opt out of Social Security."

"And military service," Holzli prodded.

"Exactly," said his father in a wary tone. "They spend most of their time looking for ways to evade social responsibilities. The Mennonites spend most of *their* time worrying about whether other people smoke and drink—slightly better, I guess, but not really full participation in the polity."

He had stopped unpacking. "Yes, and they avoid the military. Even in the war against Hitler. We had to torture some to death during the first world war, but we'd softened up by the second. Just used them in labor camps and medical experiments. Useful enough experiments, though. What happens when one goes for a while without food or water or air. Along those lines." His smile bared most of his teeth.

"He's just fooling," Holzli's mother said. "He's not in favor of that sort of thing."

"No, I'm not, but it's a good lesson in what can happen. I don't condone what was done but I understand it."

Holzli retrieved the books while they put things away. It did not rain that night, and he got far into the history book before sleep stopped him.

CHAPTER 18

It was warm walking uphill from the train station, though the sun was low and there were few clouds to hold the heat in. Holzli's scalp itched from sweat.

"Slow down!" he told the German boy with all the breath he could collect.

"We cannot. We will not be able to see for very long."

This silenced Holzli. The walk to the commuter train stop, and the tickets, and the trip itself had taken much longer than he had anticipated. He suspected it would not have taken more time to walk. Mark might be by soon, depending on his route. But, more crucial, he himself would be home very, very late.

Would his story still hold? He hoped so. His parents had been told the class was spending the afternoon at a theater on the other side of the city watching Orson Welles' version of *Macbeth*. It was a good enough dodge unless someone pressed him on details. All he knew of the movie came from stills their teacher, Mr. Reilly, had shown them. The actors looked like Mongol raiders. That would have to do for his parents.

Three weeks before, the class had made an authentic attempt to see the film. Shepherded successfully across town, they found that the theater was showing *I Married a Witch*.

It was, fortunately, something twelve-year-olds could see. Holzli's subsequent infatuation with Veronica Lake was only now dying away.

They had lost their one shot at the Welles film, but his mother and father never talked to anyone at the school. There should not have been a problem. It was already frighteningly late, however, and they had not yet done what they came to do. And there was still the trip back.

He watched for building numbers. "This must be it," he mumbled when they reached a stone house with a water trough in the tiny court before the tiny gate. There was, indeed, a plaque above the gate, almost at eye level even for them, and they stopped in the middle of the street to read it.

"Can you understand it?" Konrad asked.

"I don't know all those words."

"It says something like: 'The idea of the free church...ness...,' I guess, 'was first realized in Zollikon through the Anabaptists. In this house on January 25, 1525, one of their earliest meetings took place.'" He was quiet for a moment. "What is a 'free church?'"

"Oh, I know that from the Corbett book. It just means a church you choose to join instead of the government deciding."

"Well, then, here is where Mark got his notions. Too bad he is not here."

Holzli looked up and down the street but saw no one resembling their classmate. "Yeah, but let's go now. I'm really going to be late."

They were halfway to the Seestrasse when they met Mark.

"We have been to your plaque-house," said Konrad.

"And read your books, now." Holzli felt a joyful tension in his belly as he did sometimes when he was winning in a sport or when he chased and caught an animal. "You made this whole Regula business up."

No muscle in Mark's face so much as rippled, and that convinced Holzli they were right. Mark did not have the self-possession to hold silent before a false accusation. If he did not speak, it convicted him. It consented to any charge.

How to break what composure he did have, though, and force him to acknowledgment? Holzli stood as frozen as

Mark until the problem nearly resolved itself with no action from him. Konrad stepped up to Mark and set his hand on his shoulder—gently, intimately—and pushed the boy down.

Mark let go of his bag and put both hands behind to break his fall. He landed sitting. Something was hurt, and it showed through his face before he could force his features flat again. He brought his hands around and kneaded one wrist with the fingers of the other hand. Barely moving his mouth, he said, "I didn't make up anything."

He levered himself onto his feet with his good arm and straightened. Without dusting himself or turning, he walked past the other two and continued slowly, almost dignified, for another three meters. Then he ran.

"I have to go," Holzli said. "Now. Or I'm in trouble beyond belief."

"Angsthase, Pfeffernase..."

"I am *not*. I can only be so late and still be believed. You've got just, what, a five-minute walk?"

"More than that."

"Well, next time we'll be farther from your house and closer to the Hauptbahnhof."

"What do you mean 'next time'?"

"When we go down to where Mark saw Manz drowned."

"But he did not see Manz drowned, and we are not going there. Or, I am not."

"I'm not sure he's just lying."

Konrad lifted an eyebrow.

"No," Holzli responded. "I don't think it's true—I don't think it's as simple as a lie, though. Something about the way he acted right at the end there. It wasn't like him. He didn't fold when you pushed him and admit everything and try to laugh it off."

"What do you expect to find in the Limmat?"

"I don't know. Probably nothing. I've gotten interested in this whole Anabaptism thing, though, so I'd like to look around that area anyway."

"I would not. I am not interested in this thing and I believe Mark is lying. You will go by yourself if you go."

"At least walk with me down the hill now."

He did not know how to persuade the other. It was perfectly true that he wanted to play the tourist for reasons only indirectly tied to Mark. He wanted Konrad along, however, in case there was anything to find that bore on Mark's fantasy. He had no clue what kind of discovery that could be or how it would help if Konrad shared it. Yet, he felt the need for backup.

"Have you seen much of the historic parts of town?" he asked.

"Of course."

"Then, you'd be a pretty good guide."

"I do not remember anything. We got all of that out of the way when we first arrived so that no one could invite us later to spend the day doing it."

Holzli thought about that. "You can't have forgotten everything. Stuff will come back as you see things."

"It would if I went to see things, which I will not be doing."

Downhill was much easier on this street. Sweat evaporated from Holzli in a cold breeze that he only now noticed. He zipped his jacket up and looked around. It was perceptibly darker as well, later even than he had thought.

"How can you not be interested in this?"

"What is to be interested in? First, there is nothing downtown that shows these people existed. It is all Zwingli and the Reformers. I do not care about that. If religion mattered to me, I would study Luther, who was German.

"Second, these people sound like bourgeois anarchists."

"I don't think so."

"Well, not political. It comes to the same. If they pulled people out of society, they only got in the way of change. Or, they were...what is the word for a road that goes nowhere?"

"A dead end?"

"Yes. Even Zwingli was better."

There was no reply Holzli could make. They walked wordlessly down into the pooling shadows.

Konrad stopped so suddenly his companion thought he would fall forward. "I am not true...I mean, I did not tell the truth. I have remembered some thing: There is another plaque—it is near where Mark is talking about. It was the home of one of the leaders, I think. And something else."

"What?"

"That I will tell you after you have seen it."

"Where is it?"

"I told you."

"That's not enough to help me find it."

Konrad stared off into the grey above the buildings. "I suppose I must go with you."

CHAPTER 19

Food shops in Taiwan had an odor Holzli could not dissect. A hundred things, he supposed, came together to produce it. Swiss shops, too, all shared a smell, but he thought it reduced to cheese, and preserved meats, and coffee. He associated it with *Müesli,* too, somehow, and yogurt, but these were packaged, as was the strange milk that would not spoil at room temperature.

"*Hoi,* Holzli!" he heard behind him as he brought the groceries from the store. It was Bruno, the only authentically fat kid in his class, who liked to practice English on Holzli. He had no reason to concern himself with the language—the fourth class was too young to study it. His older brother, though, who led the *Hirsche,* the *Pfadfinder* troop, was working on it. This and the American's presence had spurred the younger boy to learn it on his own.

"Hello. How are you?" Holzli enunciated as cleanly as he could.

"How ya doin'?" Bruno returned in passably Jersey tones. Holzli did not concede responsibility for this. He had done his best to lose everything that distinguished his voice, after hearing a girl mock his German. It had not been pretty or well-meant.

Bruno, perhaps, was too talented—he caught what little escaped Holzli's guard. On the other hand, his vocabulary and grammar were growing shockingly good.

"Do you have your notebook back?" he asked. That morning, for no accessible reason, Herr Ehrlich had ripped the math notebook from under Holzli's pen. It had, in fact, been given back, tossed casually to its owner as he was leaving the room at the end of the day.

There was no marking in the book to show it had been looked at. Holzli went though it carefully for any hint of inspection and was not convinced it had even been opened.

On the last used page, he had copied

1. *Aarau zählte 39,417 Einwohner*

2. *Baden zählte 53,608 Einwohner*

3. *Bremgarten zählte 26,049 Einwohner*

4. *Laufenburg zählte funfzehntausend dreihundertvierundachtzig E.*

5. *Lenzburg zählte sechsundzwan*

There was a short stroke of ink where his pen point dragged a split second.

"Yes, it was returned." He switched them back to German. "What did he do with it?"

"I do not know. Probably nothing. I never understand what he does."

"Then, you understand as much as anyone."

The next day, while they played *Fussball* in the warming May weather, a hot air balloon crossed the sky above the valley. Someone spotted it halfway in its transit and yelled. Two boys charging at the ball from opposite sides lost their concentration and looked up long enough to meet. They both went down.

All awareness swung from the balloon to one boy who was wheezing and jerking like a landed fish. They all gathered round him with uncomprehending fright. Before the teacher could reach the knot of students, the boy calmed and sat up, breathing deliberate breaths. He had only had the wind knocked out of him.

The other boy lay unmoving and unnoticed till all were reassured about his associate. He was conscious but pale as the clouds the balloon moved against, and sweat shimmered under his eyes.

As Herr Ehrlich strode over to him, he tried to get up and clenched his face with a hiccupping noise. He lay back down and tried to reach across his chest with his right hand. Apparently, it hurt too much to twist his upper body; he waved toward himself a couple of times and gave up.

"My shoulder," he said, looking up at the teacher. "My left shoulder."

Herr Ehrlich's face could change, but only glacially. Nothing showed now. He did not incline his head. He sighted down his nose, his weight back on the heels of his thick brown shoes, his stomach pushed out against his red sweater vest. Holzli could not believe he ever changed his clothes; the heavy grey wool of his coat and cuffed trousers carried a smell only years of curing could give. It was stronger in the spring warmth.

"What is wrong with it?" the teacher asked.

The boy on the ground studied his sensations. "I think it is broken."

"Nonsense! You did not hit that hard."

Going stiffly to his knees—a concession that impressed Holzli beyond bounds—Herr Ehrlich reached under the student's pullover to probe and squeeze the shoulder. The boy sucked in his cheeks to keep from screaming, though a small sound escaped his nose.

"There is a bump here," the man said. "The bone is out of place, not broken."

He held the arm of the injured shoulder as he stood and placed a massive shoe under the armpit. "Relax and I will pull it into place."

"It was pretty awful to watch," Holzli told his mother, "But he quit after the third time. He could tell it wasn't working."

"And it wasn't dislocated?"

-112-

"No. Paul told me later it was broken and the pulling made it worse. The boy wasn't in school today."

His mother folded the dish towel she had been using and threaded it though the refrigerator handle. "This makes it easier," she said.

Holzli waited.

"We were talking to Mr. Strebel at the dinner the other night. You know—the editor at that Zürich paper."

Holzli did not know but grunted assent.

"He said this school is the worst in the Swiss school system. Actually, he also said this *village* is the worst *place* in Switzerland, but there isn't much we can do about that. He was surprised we kept you in school here this long."

A tension spread through Holzli's muscles from somewhere in his abdomen out to his extremities. He thought it might be hope, but it was delicate, barely perceptible. "So, what's going to happen?"

"Well, most of the foreign families around here live near Zürich. Some of them got together and started a school in an old mansion near the lake. A lot of them are associated with the church, so you must have met their kids."

He did know who at the church went to the school, and they were not recommendations.

"It's run by a couple the board brought in from England, and nearly all the faculty are British. The standards are supposed to be pretty high."

The children at the church thought well enough of themselves, anyway. He had never before spoken to someone and been utterly ignored, treated as a silence. It had happened to others, too, who were not in the club. Would he be a member if he started going there? He was not sure he wanted that.

"Are all the kids Americans?"

"I don't think so. It's an international enterprise. Some American companies have a big presence in the area, I guess."

His first thrill of expectation was losing what energy it had as this alternative took form. "Is it already decided?"

"We haven't been thinking about it long. I don't know what else we can arrange, though. You don't want to stay in the village school, do you? I thought you hated it."

The next full term in Zürich did not start until September. They did not want him free too long, so he would transfer for the rump end of the academic year. July and August, though, they could not take away. He looked to them as to the dawn.

He was twelve by three weeks. Money accompanied the transition, and he spent it to fortify his Beatle's collection. An album was out, *Rubber Soul,* little like the box of music from the bakery. It had been out awhile in the States and England, but he no longer cared to synchronize with other worlds. The radio could be pitiless and, these days, it inflicted the Lovin' Spoonful whenever he turned to it.

People at the new school liked that. That helped some. It gave him distance from them—ascendancy—to discover something in them to despise. The superiority was only his to see; when he publicized it, he was only the more hated.

He was consigned at once to the Canadians, Belgians, Texans, and Iranis who floated in a fringe around the social center. His father's government job did not help; it made him guilty by association for Vietnam. All the chemical people affected anti-war sentiments.

"Their fathers make napalm," Konrad told him the day they met.

"What is that?"

"It is a jellied gasoline that sticks to you and burns. They drop it on children in the war. These people's fathers invented it, and they sell it to the army. The Swiss help, somehow—I don't know if they actually make it here or just supply materials."

Holzli was willing to believe it. It implicated all the right people.

Mr. Reilly, their main teacher, an Irishman in his twenties, resented him for an intruder, coming into the middle of things. The headmaster, Mr. Austin, had made the decision after a long interview with Holzli's parents, without consulting the teacher. Holzli suspected he was serving as the target for all Mr. Reilly's bitterness toward the headmaster—much of it, he supposed, collected and nurtured for years before his own arrival.

The classwork was grim and wonderful. The grim part was algebra, which he had never met before. On the one hand, it was more entertaining than memorizing multiplication tables in German. On the other, everyone else had been doing it for a year, and Mr. Reilly was not inclined to hold him to a relaxed standard. His first morning, the teacher indicated this along with his doubts that Holzli was intelligent enough for any of the work, anyway.

Holzli's father was not sympathetic. "If you get back to the States, you'll be miles ahead of the others. American students don't get into this until high school, I think." He added his own remedial assignments, working from the beginning of the book. The boy saw the necessity, but that did not warm his mood as he sat at the kitchen divider each night, shuffling variables and listening to *The Inner Sanctum.*

The literature classes were a compensation. Holzli read the whole of the anthologies on his own within the first few days and pursued the authors beyond them. Conan Doyle's Brigadier Gerard stories drew him in for reasons he could not quite pull to the surface—something about the hero's attempts to interpret Englishmen. Shakespeare was given a regular segment of the school day to himself, when he was featured dramatically or lyrically.

If no sonnets were being looked at, time was given to other poetry. They used two volumes of a collection called the *Albemarle Book of Modern Verse.* Holzli reread his copies far into the night. Memorization had a place only here, with frequent class performances of conned lines. One student learned the whole of *Midsummer Night's Dream,* but Holzli was too entangled in the *Albemarle* to give time to plays.

Some things were determined externally. One evening, the English-speaking population of Switzerland did the same thing at the same time. Swiss television both aired a performance of *The Importance of Being Ernest* and announced it ahead of time. Why, of all the things in the world, the Wilde play was so honored, no one presumed to say. It was understood, tacitly, to be a useless question. However, the broadcast became the night's assignment for literature class, and they spent the next day discussing it.

German class was undemanding once he stopped aspirating his esses and gargling his gutturals like a local. Composition was a challenge he had, strangely, never confronted in the village school, but the woman who taught them allowed a generous range of topic and genre. Holzli liked it better than Mr. Reilly's English equivalent.

French and geography seemed unnecessary burdens, but the books were attractive. History Mr. Austin reserved as his personal domain. He ascended to them every other day and narrated without notes or props, pacing back and forth at the front of the room with his hands clasped behind his back. Some times his lessons intersected with their textbook. His grey was a different grey from Herr Ehrlich's, tweedy and tobacco-scented. Holzli was fascinated that his hair, combed straight back, rose in three rows of natural waves that never changed position, day by day.

Mr. Reilly's hair gripped his attention, too, orange like a cat's but curly. Holzli was willing to concede the color was real, but it was a forced, deliberate concession. The teacher had an aura of unpleasantness about him that repelled inspection. None of his other features registered with Holzli—five minutes after school let out, the boy could not remember what he looked like. Only the hair burned its way through, and only because of its inhuman intensity.

Mrs. Austin liked pearls and prints and pillbox hats. She taught them music in the basement where the piano was given space amidst a confusion of craft projects. Much of the floor was a diorama of a Neolithic settlement, a joint project of several classes. It had been stepped on so many times that no one had the heart to repair or complete it; the teachers themselves were too discouraged to insist.

It forced them into a tight clump around the piano where they sang from mimeographed sheets while Mrs. Austin played accompaniment. They sang "Who is Sylvia?" and "And Did Those Feet in Ancient Times," and Kipling's "Recessional." Mrs. Austin was not bothered by their complaints—she was, in fact, she said, "with it," and had enjoyed the film *Help!* immensely. It was nice that men were able to do more with their hair these days. Nevertheless, students would sing what she provided.

They only had physical education once a week, Thursdays, when they were loaded on a bus and shipped off to a monumental athletic hall, like an industrial warehouse. One entire floor, divided into two gyms with a corridor between, was reserved for a couple hours. The equipment was as old and odd as the village school's, orphaned from its time, redolent of lost days and forgotten practices. They worked with Indian clubs and worn, leather medicine balls. Afterwards, they joined the other patrons in the oceanic swimming pool on the ground level. At least once a visit, the water was replenished by sprinklers, fifteen meters up, a rain shower that made everyone pause for the moment and raise his face, eyes closed, to the ceiling.

Sometimes, they used their floor for basketball and, sometimes, they went outside for *Fussball,* which the chemical people pointedly called soccer. Konrad came into his own. He was not gracious—he taunted opponent and teammate alike, using his success as a lever to detach himself from the others. Holzli wondered how much the daily baseball games, persisted in, he discovered, unseasonably late into the year, were a response, a reaction against Europe in general and Konrad, as its representative, in particular.

One Thursday, they substituted a hike to see a glacier for the trip to the athletic hall. It rained, then, too, on the trek back down to the bus. Their sodden clothes, weighted and cold, burdened them for the rest of the day. The Centralians would not bear their loads patiently—they whined until Mr. Reilly forbade them to speak again.

Were American kids all brats? Holzli could not remember. He asked Gene, their Texan, about it as they all headed for the stairwell when class let out. A girl overheard and repeated his words, mocking his accent, and others took up the joke.

Saturdays, he was alone, now. At the heart of the village, on the street that ran between the school and the post office, a bridge crossed over the river and fastened the town together. He liked to lean on the black, iron railing and watch the surface of the water undulate downstream. He dropped sticks and leaves and followed them with his eyes into the invisible distance toward the Rhine. The great river took them to the sea.

All the other children should have been incarcerated behind and to his right. "Holzli! How goes it?" someone said from that direction, and Holzli straightened with a startled jerk. Paul stood behind him.

Was school letting out early? Holzli turned to the yard near the butcher shop where the doors let out that the students were supposed to use. It was empty and he heard no voices. He noticed, now, that Paul had no backpack.

"No school today?" he asked.

"No, it is a holiday." Paul was not looking at him. Holzli turned again and found Bruno approaching from the post office.

"Why are you no longer attending our school?" Paul asked as they waited for the other boy to reach them.

"I am sorry, I do not understand. "

Bruno arrived, and Paul tried again. "Why have you stopped coming to school here in the village?"

"I still do not understand."

"He is asking why you are no longer coming to our school," Bruno asked in English.

"I know what he is asking. I do not want to answer."

"I do not know enough to translate for you," Bruno told Paul, who shrugged.

They all leaned over the railing and watched the water.

CHAPTER 20

They decided they would need a Saturday to poke around the Grossmünster, and Holzli had his lie prepared: he would tell his parents precisely where he meant to go but cast it as another class trip. The latter element would not work too much more often; he could only hope no genuine trips were planned.

He delayed saying anything and, then, late on Thursday, he fell ill. When they had first arrived and were living in the hotel, he caught some virus that laid him out more sick than he had ever been in his life. It did not last long. He awakened in the dark predawn in sheets so wet with sweat they might just have been washed—his fever had broken spectacularly. He had read about this but, as he did with many things in books, he had consigned it to another world, a parody of this one, with its own peculiar, irrelevant phenomena.

The first few months, he was hit hard by every bug that came visiting. Nothing like this had happened in Taiwan; he had dysentery, but that was carelessness, not contagion. Time in Europe strengthened something in him, however, and his health had been untroubled by outside forces till now.

His parents were not easily sent running to doctors, and he was glad. He had one experience with a local pediatrician and it inoculated him against desire for another visit. A wart on his finger had grown big enough that he could not use his hand without irritating it. It was inflamed and sore. The doctor examined it and decided to carve it out. To anesthetize the finger, he brought out a hypodermic so large Holzli thought, at first, it had to be a prop of some kind. It looked antique, with circles for the first two fingers to hold against the pressure of the thumb. The needle itself was two centimeters long, of dreadful gauge.

Holzli would not extend his hand to be treated, and the doctor had limited patience. After a third try to coax the boy into compliance, he turned to paperwork and left things to the mother.

"You're disgracing yourself," she said. "The soldiers in Vietnam have to put up with a lot worse than that every day. You can't act like this in front of foreigners."

Only the first couple of millimeters of the needle were used. There was no sensation after that—the cutting was a spectacle, not an experience. Holzli laughed to see the stagnant blood, exactly like the ink they used in school, welling out and into the cracks and rills of the palm.

"He laughs," the doctor noted. He did not sound amused himself.

"Don't overdo it," whispered Holzli's mother. "You don't want to sound forced."

Friday, he stayed home and hoped Konrad would guess the plans were off.

"Where were you?" the German asked on Monday.

"When?"

"Saturday. I waited for you at the Bahnhof until noon."

"I was sick! I wasn't here Friday! Why would you think we were still meeting?"

"You did not say we were cancelled. Why would I assume that?"

"I *couldn't* tell you. I wasn't here."

"You should have used the telephone."

"That would just be a big mess. I'd have to find your number, and I'd have to come up with a reason for my parents for calling you, and I'd have to figure out how to call without them overhearing!"

"So, instead, you let me come into the city and wait in the train station."

Nothing was to be achieved by continuing in this direction. Holzli and the other boy had been down similar paths before.

"What about next Saturday? If I don't..."—he fumbled for the word—"*confirm* it on Friday, you can assume it's off."

It took until Friday for Konrad to relent. "Okay," he said, then. "But I will only wait for you between eleven and twelve—whatever trains come in that time—and then I leave!"

He was standing halfway down the platform when the train pulled in. Holzli saw him flash by his window and hurried to jump out before he was carried too far past.

Konrad was so intent on the few doors near him that the other boy was able to tag him, hard, between the shoulder blades with his palm. "Shit!" he grunted, stumbling toward the train before reclaiming his balance. "Do not do that! What do you think you are up to?"

The abrupt anger stole Holzli's own balance. "Uh, you're it, I guess."

"Whatever that is supposed to mean." Konrad's upper body was one clenched muscle as though only so could he keep himself from hitting back.

"Sorry," said Holzli, hoping that would thaw him, melt the rigidity and get him moving. There was not much time and he did not want to spend any of it on emotional management.

"Let us just go," said Konrad and began to walk stiffly to the steps.

A few minutes in the cold sunshine softened him to conversation. "One thing that I did notice in the Keller book is that he thinks only married women wore scarves wrapped around their heads."

"So what?"

"Well, did not Mark say his Regula had such a scarf?"

"I don't know. Was that in the part you told me?"

"Whether it was or not, Mark did say it."

"Then it's another thing we can ask him about. Why are you turning here?"

"Why should we cross the bridge? This is the side that the guy would have been drowned from. We can cross over farther down."

At the next bridge down, they left traffic behind. The Bahnhofquai stopped and they had to make their way through cobblestone alleys.

"You have seen the Lindenhof, is that not true?"

"Yeah," answered Holzli. "What there is to see. We don't need to go up there now, do we?"

"Oh, no. But, if I am to be tour guide, I am obligated to disclose possibilities."

They were almost to another bridge and, across the water, abutting the bridge to its north, was a flat, concrete platform.

Holzli waved the other's attention that way. "That must be what Mark was talking about. The place that juts into the water. It's not quite straight across from the Lindenhof. But that would mean Manz was drowned out in the middle there."

"I don't see any building out there."

"Corbett says one was there. That's all Mark needs for support. I don't remember that he described anything very well."

"Does it not seem to you," Konrad asked when they had watched the water for a time, "that there is a swirling out in the middle? As though something is underneath there?"

"Maybe. But I can't see very deep that far out."

"If you climb the tower of the Grossmünster, you can see the bottom of the river. Unless this is too distant. We should try."

They poked around on their side a bit, finding nothing pertinent, and angled their way onto the bridge.

"Oho!"

Holzli had been looking down into the water, remembering the ice that had been there the first time he saw it. If Manz' January had been like his, he could not have drawn a breath, water or no. Konrad's cry snapped his thoughts off.

"What are you 'Oho'ing about?" he asked, irritated.

"You said he did not describe anything very well. He did give us one detail that he must have thought made the story better. He told us he discovered they were selling fish here. But he must have known that! This is called the Fish Market Bridge. If he has spent any time here at all, he knows that."

Somehow, Holzli could not match his glee. The game was growing sad. Each chip they knocked out of Mark's construction was more decisive for him. He supposed he no longer believed any of it, and that narrowed the world, robbed it of potential. He did not follow Konrad, who was crossing without looking behind. Instead, he stared back into the water. His guide was on the other side before he noticed Holzli had not followed. "What are you doing there? What do you see?"

Holzli turned his head and opened his mouth to respond but could not think of anything that deserved saying. Slowly, without energy, he unbent and headed toward the east bank.

Konrad did not wait for him. Holzli did not expect him to. The German boy went down around to Mark's platform and made a show of inspecting the posts that poked up from the river. "Nothing to see here," he said when Holzli arrived.

"What is that building there?"

"I have no idea," said Konrad. "But look—on the other side of the bridge."

They walked around to the south of the bridge. A building there extended symmetrically with Mark's platform.

"The Rathaus. The old Council House. Do you want to look at it?"

"I guess not."

"What I want to show you is close to here, only a few blocks. It would make sense to go there first and then to the Grossmünster.

"Fine. But you're not going to tell me what it is."

"No, and I cannot remember the Anabaptist's name. You will see from the plaque. That is not what makes it interesting, though."

They threaded a narrow street uphill for several blocks before hitting a main street.

"We have overshot. We will have to follow this and hope the right street comes off of it."

They shed some altitude before Konrad said, "This is called the Neumarkt Street, so it must go where we want."

"Here's something," Holzli called out a minute later.

"That is not it. That is—hah! It tells that Gottfried Keller was born here."

"Okay. Let's keep moving."

When they came to a triangular intersection, Konrad said, "This is the place. And there is the house '*Zur Eintracht*.'"

"To what?"

"'To Harmony.' Go read the plaque."

This one read: "In this house lived, 1508-1514 and 1520-1525, Konrad Grebel who, together with Felix Manz, started Anabaptism."

"So, Grebel," said Holzli. "The big one." He noted the "K" in the name, but was not about to mention it, and there was little else to say. He ran his sight over the face of the building but nothing stood out. "Thanks—but what is the other interesting thing about this?"

Konrad's smile was wider and more genuine than any Holzli had seen on him. He swept his arms in grand signification. "Lenin lived here. Vladimir Lenin. During the war, right before he returned to Russia."

"Cool." Holzli was impressed but, again, there was little else to say once the fact had been acknowledged.

The other's disappointment in him was plain—the smile guttered out. Still, strain as he might, he could express nothing but another "Cool."

"Perhaps we shall pass on to the big church." Konrad's voice, too, had lost something it had just a moment before.

They continued in the same direction till Konrad said, "We need not return to the river. We can slant off here." He motioned into an alley they were passing.

"But it's not the route Mark took."

"He said nothing about the way between—it does not matter how we arrive. Let us not waste time."

That made sense, but Holzli knew it was no kin to the other boy's true motives. The tone revealed that. Konrad wanted to go down the alley only because Holzli was already beyond its mouth. He would be compelled to walk back to Konrad.

"We don't know what he saw. Anything might be important. It's not that far anyway. We should try to repeat the order he saw things in." Even as he spoke, he realized both that his reasoning was no stronger than Konrad's and that it did not matter. The point, he was suddenly aware, was to avoid the real issues.

Still, the matter could be forced if not acknowledged. "I'm going on this way, back by the Rathaus. You can do whatever you want. I've already seen what you were going to show me. I can do the rest by myself if you don't want to come along."

Konrad stood, his thumbs in this pockets, with no sign of moving, so Holzli went on. Going no faster than appearances obliged, he was halfway to the Limmatquai before he could be sure that was Konrad in the corner of his vision.

"And here is yet another plaque," he said, but got no response. "Oh, God! This is Gottfried Keller's childhood home! The Kellers must have liked the neighborhood. Keep going! *Schnell!*"

Even this provoked nothing.

They could see the water and the reddish-brown tile roofs on the other side before he tried again.

"How did you find out that was Lenin's house?" he asked. He did not care, but he had to offer some concession.

"My father told me."

At the river again, they headed south. Looking at the shops fronting the street slowed them, but they came to yet another bridge and a church that blocked their progress.

"I don't remember what this is," said Konrad. "That's the Grossmünster over there." Across the street to their left, up steps to another level, was a larger, spired structure.

"Mark would have run into this, coming the other way. Let's go around."

On the other side was something the American recognized at once. He had seen it in the shop window in Einsiedeln. Zwingli, with his Bible and sword, ignored them from his pedestal, gazing far above their heads.

"No getting anything from that one," Konrad observed. "We may as well move on."

Holzli made a sound of assent but continued to look up at the stone man. After a moment, a piece of gravel bounced off the figure and there were shouts all around.

He turned to see that Konrad had put on his tight smile. "Did you throw that? What did you do that for?"

"Now we must definitely move on," was Konrad's only response. He ran a few paces toward the street, swiveled to beckon, and took off again.

Holzli followed at speed, not wanting to be left to face the mob. A car had already halted, still honking reprimands at Konrad, and Holzli made it across without pausing. He chased the other boy along the walk and up the steps into a plaza.

Both were panting when the lead runner finally stopped and waited to be overtaken. Holzli spoke as his breath allowed: "What...the...hell?"

"I...wanted to see...if I might get his attention...It did not work."

They stood and heaved until he could say more. "We are out of shape. That was not very far. We are now, however, in the presence of a church built by Karl der Grosse himself—'Charlemagne' in lesser tongues. There he is now." He pointed to a statue in one of the spires. "Martyrs are buried somewhere underneath—I do not remember their story. The doors might tell us something."

"Wait, I was thinking back there—before we had to leave. The very first thing Mark saw that day when he walked up here must have been Ulrich there. He's pretty impressive. Mark must have started working on his story right then. It kicked it off anyway. Then, the rest of what he saw that day must have reminded him of things from Corbett."

"Unless he read the book later. But, I suppose, the plaque near his house might have got him interested in the Reformation and he might have come across the Corbett book searching for information in the library. And, yes, you are right—this certainly is where the idea for the lie came from."

The big, paneled doors were tarnished bronze. "Actually, they are recent. From earlier this century," Konrad noted.

"And Mark told me, at least, that he spent time looking at them."

A large, cardboard placard, stapled on a wooden sawhorse and curled by rain, stood to the doors' right and explained each panel in a corresponding square.

"They're mostly about Zwingli."

"Yes, that is the point of them. But about Zürich, too. See, at the bottom on the left are the martyrs and on the right we have, again, Charlemagne. The martyrs were Zürich's patron saints when one could have such things. They are also in the canton's coat of arms—up at the top there."

"You couldn't remember their names."

"No."

"Do you see what they are? Felix and Exuperantius and Regula! He just lifted the girl's name from here!"

"It would not be odd for a girl to be named after the local saint."

"No, but I bet Mark wasn't thinking that much. He was just too lazy to come up with another name."

"Well, another thing to throw in his face."

Holzli nodded as he scanned the other panels. Nothing else was as good. The sun was still high and bright, and he liked that for once. He relaxed under the warmth on his neck, perceiving suddenly how near he had been to a headache. It would have launched a migraine. All tension liquefied and flowed away.

"Is there anything to see south of here?"

"I cannot think of anything, but you should really see inside. We can go up the tower and down into the crypt."

"Can we save that for another day?" He felt, somehow, too light for anything intentional.

"Okay. But I have remembered just one more thing you must see. Inside. Very cool."

Holzli was led to where he recognized the altar had once been. It struck him that the Catholics would have filled this building with color. That must have been the first thing the Reformers changed, and now all was stone and shadows.

"Here, on the wall."

"Well, that's Jesus, but what's around him?"

"There is an executioner's axe. And that is a, I think you say, cat with nine tails. And there is a scourge, and a club, and a spear. And some sort of darts. Tools for Christians to use."

Holzli knew he would normally have been shocked, but right now he just felt warm and insulated from everything. The instruments could not penetrate—they were no matter for concern. "I'm just going to walk back to the Bahnhof. It's too nice a day not to. I'll go all the way up the Limmatquai."

His companion seemed to see a strangeness in him and released him without comment, unaccompanied. He made the trip back to the village through a weightless country, through luminous, vividly colored landscapes without substance. Void himself, he floated through a hollow, buoyant world, free and happy. Was it the sun or some other element of the day? He did not know and could not bring himself to care.

Home, his debriefing on the class trip behind him, he took his *Lives of the Saints* from the shelf and fell onto the bed. There was no Regula in the list of saints, but he found the name in the index. It led him to a section called "St. Maurice and His Companions" and a surprise:

> "St. Maurice (St. Moritz, St. Mauritius) commanded the Theban Legion, a unit of the Roman Army composed of Christians from Upper Egypt. He is typically portrayed as black in iconography. Led by the Emperor Maximian as part of a force to suppress an uprising of Gauls, the Legion encamped near Agaunum, the modern Swiss town of St.-Maurice-en-Valais, after the victory. The Emperor then gave orders that all units were to sacrifice Christian prisoners as thanksgiving offerings to the gods. Upon the Theban Legion's refusal to participate, they were twice 'decimated' and, after continued defiance, executed to a man...A number of the legion's members were absent at the time of the executions. These were subsequently located and put to death. Sts. Felix, Regula and Exuperantius

(Exuperantus) were apprehended in Zürich and beheaded on the site of today's Water Church on the banks of the Limmat. According to legend, they then picked up their heads and carried them a short distance uphill to a spot on which Charlemagne later founded another church in their honor. This was the predecessor of the famous Grossmünster, seat of the Swiss Reformation."

"Regula" was a *guy's* name? There did not seem any way around it. Holzli laughed till the muscles in his temples hurt, threatening the headache he had escaped.

He envied the saints their decapitation. It would amputate his chief source of suffering. But how would he respond to the sight of the blade? He assumed the martyrs had met it with iron faces. They were soldiers and saints in the presence of their enemies and not at liberty to flinch. If he could not match their composure, he was neither soldier nor saint. What role, then, was open to him? Those exhausted the worthy possibilities.

So much always seemed to hang on how one faced pain.

CHAPTER 21

In the night, grey clouds budded and blossomed and grew until, by morning, they choked out the sky. A muted, pearly light percolated through but only showed that snow was coming. Autumn had surrendered with little struggle. Cold was sweeping in—the temperature kept dropping until early afternoon. As they drove back from the city, they met lone white flakes that turned to spots of water on the windshield.

Early snows brought Holzli something like the melancholy bliss of rain, and only late in winters did he completely change allegiance, rebelling against the season's restriction and looking to spring for green deliverance. For now, the swelling grey above promised its own dark release. It held him rapt, anticipating whatever it was hiding in its billows.

Rain he had had to satiety in Taipei. Snow he had gone without the whole two years, except as the distant, pale tip of a mountain. When the thermometer fell below 20° C and sweaters were brought out and roasted yams were sold on the roadsides, he had strained for the smell of snow in the breezes. Sometimes, he thought he caught traces from far off—blown down from Siberia or Hokkaido or the Aleutians, perhaps—but never strong and never his.

Autumn, there, had been only a change in the light. Here, it had all the force one could ever wish. And today it was not subtle in its leaving. He did not expect it back.

They did their civic duty, walking the road above the house, as the snow closed in, heavier and colder. Unwrapping in his room, looking forward to an afternoon of snowbound leisure, he noticed his attaché case on the desk and remembered all that was due the next day. At once, everything was ruined.

He had not meant to turn on the radio—there was a mood to the day that would be broken by the sound. Yet, the alternative was to open the case, and he could not steel himself to that. What, however, was least intrusive? The pirate station offered things the armed forces did not. The Rolling Stones, for instance, had come to full growth outside the latter's ken. But the pirates did not appreciate Detroit enough.

In the end, it did not matter. The day itself refused to be disturbed; something about the weather was blocking reception. He cycled through squeals and sputters for a time, caught a fleeting, cloudy snatch of The Four Tops, then clicked the thing off.

There was a way to get started. It would not obligate him to begin at once if he simply dumped the case's contents on the bed. If that was all he set himself to do for now, he could bring himself to act.

The second Albemarle volume fell out with the other things, and, normally, it would have been the one good item in the dreary heap. Now, it only modeled the worst assignment of the lot: to write a poem in the style of e. e. cummings.

Corbett's cardboard packaging caught his notice. That was the instrument of delay he needed. He pushed everything else to the foot of the bed and sat and rolled the rubber band from the book. It was losing its integrity—each time he read it, more pages separated from the rest. Only his own regard kept it a whole.

The book therefore had no biases and could fall open anywhere. He preferred the narratives—the history and the anecdotes—but he only got a short one this time:

> "A favorite illustration of this response is the account of Dirk Willems from *The Martyrs*

Mirror. In 1569, in Asperen, Holland, Willems was pursued across thin ice by an agent of the burgomaster. He himself crossed safely but, looking back, saw that his pursuer had fallen through into the water. He returned and rescued the drowning man, whereupon he was arrested and handed over for execution. While he was being burned, a strong east wind kept the fire from his upper body, prolonging his ordeal.

"The early Anabaptists embraced the martyr tradition of the Church as much by necessity, however, as by conviction. Repudiating coercive force as a social instrument, they both put themselves outside normal social structures and left themselves highly vulnerable to the consequences.

"This nonresistance to evil, grounded in Christ's injunction of *Matthew* 5:39, is commonly seen as the distinctive feature of the movement, but it was originally one thread in a larger fabric of belief. Since most of the other major tenets have lost their controversial force, it is often hard to understand the importance assigned them by all parties of the time."

Holzli flipped ahead to determine how long this part would last and saw no end coming soon. Outside, the wind was rising, but the thick, concrete walls and newly fitted storm windows with their pelt-like drapes made the house a fortress. He went to his window and shouldered the heavy material aside. The snow was falling down densely now and piled up where it fell. It was so dark the sun's setting would make scant difference.

He returned and found his place:

"The practice of adult, or believer's, baptism, if not accepted by all denominations, has no power to shock us now. In the sixteenth century, it was deemed worth killing or dying for. This becomes more plausible once we reflect on the historical context and the prevailing relation between Church and State.

"In a world where political jurisdictions were all expressly 'Catholic' or 'Protestant,' citizenship and sectarian loyalty were inseparable phenomena. To be the citizen of a particular state was to be a member of a particular church and vice versa. Baptism, as a symbol of entry into a Christian community, thus had the derivative function of signifying one's adoption of a political identity. It marked the moment at which one assumed membership in a secular community. Of course, if one was baptized as an infant, no real choice was involved."

Holzli flipped forward again. There were sixteen pages to the end of this chapter. Then came another round of persecutions. He considered jumping ahead to that, but it would be too wimpy. If Dirk Willems could stand being roasted slowly alive, he himself could tolerate a few more pages of this.

"For the Anabaptists, a legal requirement of infant baptism implied the superiority of the State over human will—of the earthly over the divine. Their insistence that only an adult's conscious choice could lead to meaningful baptism effectively severed the tie between public and spiritual allegiance. Further, because their rejection of force made it impossible for them to participate in government, baptism became precisely a sign of separation from the political community, not membership in it. They saw themselves as subject to the government's just demands but not as participating citizens."

This he found interesting but tiring. The following pages seemed to be more of the same, but he turned a couple and dove in again.

"Debates in Anabaptist circles between moral legalists and what we might call 'moral spiritualists' paralleled the disputes over narrow, literal interpretation of scripture versus freer, more 'spiritual' and inspired readings. There was no strict correlation between an individual's position on one and the other issue. In the end, however, the legalist and literalist approaches proved to be stronger supports for the nonresistant stance and they have historically been the dominant tendencies in Anabaptist thought. This is, perhaps, unfortunate, but it is understandable that constant opposition would force these groups into defensive, inflexible positions merely to hold together and survive with their principles intact.

"In all periods and under all constructions, the Christian's relation to the broader political world has been the defining concern for the Anabaptists. This has been due less to their own choosing than to the responses of others, but that itself is telling. Unless one rejects their premises radically, one may be compelled to the conclusion that Christianity is political in its essence, if only in the breach."

He shaped the book into an even rectangularity and replaced the rubber band. The cummings poems in their collection were short enough, anyway. Starting now, he should have something acceptable by suppertime.

CHAPTER 22

The morning was arctic. His trips down the hill to the bus stop had been lightless and frigid for weeks. When he had a clear sky it was easier to see but colder—all warmth was lost up into the black between the lights. Now, there was snow to fight as well, and it would be there every morning, trapping his boots with every step. It granted one advantage: he was hot enough to open his coat before he reached the village.

He was not awake enough to deal with this. Had there been more hours to recover from the night he could have girded up his emotional loins, braced himself for the plunge into the icy darkness and the unpleasantness of the day that waited on the other side. However, he found there was another benefit to the struggle with the snow. He could focus on each labored step, blocking out all that hovered about the periphery of his awareness—thoughts of other times and other places—isolating himself in this one event, the lift and fall of his leg. He did not like here and now, but the moment was finite and contained. Nothing worse could enter.

But when his concentration faltered, he remembered that the day might hold two good things. Konrad and he could settle with Mark once and for all—rip out his story by its roots and fling it in his face.

This might also be the day that the next number of the new German *Superman* comic book arrived at the Bahnhof kiosk. It was getting past time. He had spotted the first issue by chance, two months before, looking through sports magazines while waiting for the train. The series was published in Stuttgart and, judging by the list of prices on the cover, shipped to every German-speaking population in Europe.

Reading that first copy had been like going back to the 1930's and catching the narrative in the germ, brand new. All the decades of associations were gone and the whole thing was starting over. For the first time, Mutter and Vater Kent discovered the alien child in the field and adopted him as their own. Now, long before George Reeves, Clark Kent found a job as a reporter for the *Planeten-Rundschau,* a great metropolitan newspaper. The world was being built anew, panel by panel. What was that up in the sky? *Ein Vogel? Ein Düsenjäger? Nein,* it was Superman!

Why not *Übermensch?* That was what Konrad said was the proper translation. That there should already be a settled translation was strange, but the term apparently had broader, unknown applications even in English. The Donovan song, "Sunshine Superman," for instance, had no easy connection with the comic book character.

There was no wind, a blessing in the long minutes until the bus came; the shelter had only formal existence. It was not long before he zipped his coat closed again. Cars passed at intervals, crunching through snow that had collected again on the cleared roadway.

Donovan's "Season of the Witch" was actually a better song and it resisted interpretation more than the other. The song lyrics in popular music were increasingly obscure at the same time they gained in interest. The music itself had improved by a leap, he thought, just in the past year. It all had to be connected somehow.

The city had been hit as hard as the northern hills. As on rainy days, they were free, during lunch and the break, to find what diversion they could in the mansion, but the snow drew everyone to the park.

Somehow, when routine vanished in the snow, it took all distinctions and exclusions with it. Holzli and Konrad, however, only joined in the main battle long enough to cut Mark out of the crowd. Alternating their throws, they drove him back behind the great elm, away from the others.

"Stop it!" he demanded with a faltering smile, unsure in what spirit to take their attack. He had managed to snatch up enough snow to make a ball but did not want to use it against one and have no threat left against the other.

"Okay," said Holzli. "We will. Put down your snowball first."

Mark was wary of Konrad, who stayed back by the tree, tossing a missile from hand to hand.

"Make Konrad drop his!"

"No, you drop yours first. You're not in a position to bargain."

A grey bunting of cloud hung motionless, frozen, over the lake. Breaking the new snow, Mark began sidling toward Holzli. The latter did not see the ball fall from Mark's hand, but Konrad did and charged. Mark tried to back suddenly, but his feet were caught. He stayed up, hopping, until his assailant reached him with his own snowball and pushed it into his face. Grabbing Konrad's collar, he still kept himself from going down. Holzli lifted a wedge of snow with both hands and dumped it on Mark's head, patting the shards into the boy's coat and shirt.

Mark spun away from Konrad and struck Holzli's chin with a looping hand. He continued his arc down onto his knees and looked up immediately.

The blow did not hurt. Holzli picked up more snow and sprinkled it on the kneeling boy. "Like sand in a litter box, so are the days of our lives."

"What is that supposed to mean?" asked the German.

"Never mind. He recognizes it. And thinks it's funny. Don't you?"

"No," answered Mark. He waited passively for more to happen, then asked, "What do you assholes want?"

"We took a little trip downtown," Holzli started. He looked to Konrad, who said nothing. "We know where you got all your ideas for your stupid stories."

Between the two of them, they related their tour and conclusions. "There is nothing in what you say that would not be suggested by what we saw," finished Konrad. "You started thinking it up during that one walk."

"And none of the other parts wouldn't have come from books," added Holzli.

"And you got things wrong."

"And 'Regula' is a man's name, not a woman's. That was the dumbest part."

They stared at Holzli blankly. Slowly, expressions took hold—nasty glee on one and indignation on the other. Mark's bottom lip puffed out, and a soft sound emerged, like a wind's whisper. While he labored to turn this to words, he puffed and reddened so much Holzli feared something would burst.

"Wh...what are you talking about?"

"You got the name off the doors of the church, but you didn't check to see who the real Regula was. He was a Roman soldier."

"That's ridiculous! I didn't get the name from anywhere! It's her name."

"This is excellent," Konrad commented. "Also pathetic. Do not talk to us any more about this Regula."

"Yeah, just let it die." Holzli took a step in the direction of the school, then had a thought. "Tell you what. Ask Regula what she knows about *Hornussen*. If she's really from the old days, she'll know what it is and you can tell us. We'll believe anything you say then."

"What...*Hornussen?* Is it a joke?"

"Of course it's a joke, you putz! We're never going to believe anything you say again, regardless."

"Hey! Retards!" They all looked up at Alison Hopper, whose father was the most important of the chemical execs, and her main flunky, Debby Petersen. Alison had long assumed the burden of supervising behavior, even for those who would be beneath her notice in the normal course of things. "In case you haven't figured it out, break is over. Everyone else is going in."

"Well, great, Alison. Thanks for letting us know."

The girls continued to glare with flat, reptilian intensity.

"Why do you not go ahead in, and we will follow in a moment?" tried Konrad.

"If you're not in on time, we all get in trouble."

"Yeah, big trouble," said Mark. "Mr. Reilly might tell us not to be late next time."

The boys regarded him with astonished admiration, but Debby said, "Just get yourselves in, you morons." She and Alison turned and walked away with nearly military coordination. There was nothing to do but follow, though this was the semblance of obedience.

There was no new *Superman,* but, searching for it, he uncovered something equally as good. He had not even known a German series of *Classics Illustrated* existed, and here was H. G. Wells' *Die Zeitmaschine* hidden behind a French aviation magazine. It even had the feel and texture of the American version, instead of the slick paper that struck him as a false note in the other comic. He ransacked the kiosk's racks until the proprietor growled at him. There were no others; still, he had the one and carried it off with him to the train.

He could read by the yellow bulbs above the seats. Outside, everything rattled by in the night that fell now before he left the station. The book on which this was based had been a favorite once, read and reread almost to memorization. Examining a panel that showed a future landscape in the rain, he understood all of a sudden why he had wanted Mark's inventions to be true. It was not simply that he wanted a way left open to wonder—he wanted time freed from its channel, from its fixed and downward flow. If only Mark were not a liar, all could be gotten back and all could be made right. The whole course of things could always be turned. Nothing would be forever set and nothing forever lost.

He let pages flutter through his fingers. Some places out there must be the fields he passed in daylight. There were no house or street lights; the train might as well be shooting through a void. They clattered and jerked, and the bulbs flickered, then held steady, then went out. In the darkness, he could not feel the progress of the train, only the sway from side to side and the loss and gain of weight when they hit bumps. The lights came on again and he bent down to upturned Morlock faces.

CHAPTER 23

Sports should have supplied continuity. They were limited little worlds whose histories flowed smoothly. Ages before, he had been to an Eagles game and followed them thereafter until his life made it too unnatural.

The Armed Forces station had relayed games in Taiwan, and he assumed they would here, but it was clear that, even in this realm, things were changing fast. In June, it was announced that there was to be a championship game between the two leagues in January, a sort of World Series of football, and it was hinted that the AFL was headed for absorption by its rival. Whole continents were shifting.

Late in the month, he was abruptly free. The afternoon was spent watching a filmed production of *Pirates of Penzance*. Mrs. Austin had been promising it for weeks and finally persuaded Mr. Reilly to give her the class for this last day. They ended with a party and got out early—they nearly all escaped the stairwell before the final bell filled it with echoes from the crowning dome.

Outside, under a sun unthreatened by clouds for the first time Holzli remembered, those who wanted made their goodbyes. Most would spend their summer together anyway, in Zürich or in Michigan. Konrad and he dawdled before the gate, speculating about the next year's teaching assignments. It almost certain Mr. Hughes, the Welshman, would have their class. They watched Mark leave the building and head toward the side gate. He saw them and started to change direction, but they waved dismissal and he went on. That gave them their own occasion for parting, however, and they could set off home with little further fuss.

Two months and more were Holzli's to consume as he pleased. He read that night till early morning without plan, grazing among the books stored up on his shelves against an opportunity like this. With no demands on his time, he could not focus; he finished the first story of an anthology and put the book back on its pile. Evading duty, apparently, had lent a savor to things only appreciated in its absence.

What to read? Sleep was not an alternative yet. He scanned the room. All he had used in school was stacked on a corner of the desk—he was scarcely that desperate. It was a meager enough collection for all the drudgery it had entailed. The relics from the village school came to less, though, and stood for greater suffering. Those were on the lowest level of a bookcase, horizontal with their spines against the wall.

Most were notebooks. He had not opened them in the two months since he left, but now a late-night nostalgia ran through him like a chill and he got down to pull the pile out. On top was the yellowish-brown volume that held his notes from religion class.

The students had reproduced them verbatim from the board, along with the instructor's illustrations. Holzli understood the language now, as he had not early on, and he could see where he must have copied letters wrong.

The early lessons had been the Ten Commandments, one Commandment per week. The notes were largely outlines and summaries of the instructor's lectures, though both he and the students had spent a lot of time drawing and coloring the pictures.

Here, too, time brought comprehension. He saw how the long discussion of modern African slavery was supposed to relate to the Eighth Commandment. *Das 8. Gebot,* the page was headed. *Du sollst nicht stehlen.* Then he had copied: "The original meaning of this Commandment is: Thou shalt steal no man. God wants, therefore, to protect human freedom." In the middle of the page he had sketched what appeared to be two camels of different species leaving an inflatable, backyard wading-pool. The rest of the page was about Joseph's sale into slavery.

He wished he had understood better and been able to ask questions. As it was, this interpretation would be forever opaque and weird. The religion classes had stopped, however, when he left for Zürich.

The rest of the stack just depressed him. What else, then? There was his *Pfadfinder Büchlein,* his Boy Scout handbook, small and brown with a Mountie hat and a pennant with a deer totem like his own *Hirsche* troop's. It reminded him that there was one planned and settled element to his summer; the week in Graubünden had been scheduled for months. His broken dagger sat on the bureau next to the stiff, leather belt with its scabbard and funny, interlocking metal buckle. If only he had not spoiled the thing—it could have been his proudest possession.

He slept, finally, too much a creature of rhythm to put it off too long. In the next nights, however, he made it farther and farther toward morning and, at length, remained awake to see each daybreak. When the floor lit up red under the drapes, he would creep out of his room, ease the front door open and closed, and climb the hill behind the house until he could see the dawn, unobstructed, to the east.

The sun and he stood above the roads and buildings, facing each other across the depths between the mountain heights. Having escaped all routine, beyond convention and—almost—nature, he felt, in those instants, on the verge of leaving time.

But only on the verge, and the opportunities did not last. His parents wanted to travel and wanted him back in a normal sleeping pattern, and the two aims coincided.

His father could get days off at a time but seldom with much advance notice. They suited their trips to the time allowed. Short ones took them to the bears of Bern and the squirrels of Arosa. The longer ones took them over the borders on all sides.

Holzli fell into an infatuation with Liechtenstein. It started when he learned it was the last of the Holy Roman Empire, but the country's size and modesty appealed. When they ate, the straw for his drink was actually a hollow section of straw, answering a question he had never thought to ask. He began formulating long-range plans to change his citizenship.

Baden-Württemberg was on the edge of sight from their house, but its neighbor Bavaria was more thoroughly explored. His father's job somehow gave him access to Army facilities and privileges, and the German south was sprinkled with American bases. The family did not use these often, and Holzli prized them all the more for that. They were his only chance for hamburgers and milkshakes. In school, they talked about Wimpy's restaurants, but you had to go even farther for those—to England—and reports were mixed. Europeans, moreover, generally had Northeasterner's notion of a shake; for a frappe, one needed an American military base.

Comic books could be gotten, too, in limited fashion. Most had continuing plots, which did Holzli no good. He had been interested in seeing what Batman was like, since America was reportedly obsessed with a television show about him, but nothing was available. That left comics about World War II, and he bought a few until a moment in Berchtesgaden took all joy from them.

Just to stay there, they broke a day of travel off early on their way to Austria. "You'll get a kick out of this place," his father told them, tugging the parking brake a third time for certainty's sake. "They call it the Hotel General Walker, but, before the Army took it over at the end of the war, it was the Hotel Platterhof. Hitler made this area his holiday retreat because he stayed in the Platterhof in the 'twenties and liked it. Registered as 'Mr. Wolf.' Wrote *Mein Kampf* here, in fact."

He twisted to address his son as he opened his door. "Maybe in your very room. You could meet his ghost! Or, if you don't get the right room, you might meet him in the bathroom—the rooms don't have showers and toilets. You have to go down the hall. Increases your odds of using a toilet the Führer himself used."

As soon as Holzli was settled into his room, he returned to the reception hall and hunted up the PX. The same selection as always was on tap—he finally, as always, chose an issue of a combat series.

Two figures were on the cover: American and *Wehrmacht* soldiers. The American stood on the bank of a river, in the shadows under a bridge, holding his M1 at his hip, his knees bent as though bracing to charge. The other stood near the mouth of the river tunnel, screened by the corner, a potato-masher grenade at the end of his extended arm, ready for a throw. The words "Here's a gift for you, Yankee pig!" floated in a balloon above the Nazi's head. The American's balloon held: "Come on in! The water's fine!"

Holzli handed the book to a balding, sad-eyed man behind the cashier's counter. "That will be twelve cents," the man informed him in a German accent.

The boy handed him a dollar in red scrip. The clerk dug for change in the register and began to count it out, but looked down at the cover of the magazine and paused. He examined Holzli's face. "They do not talk to each other," he said.

Back in the room, the comic just seemed silly. Holzli threw it away when he was finished.

The trips ended in July when he went to the *Pfadfinder* camp, and only one thing more marked the summer. On the first day of August, the village celebrated National Day, Swiss Independence Day, with fireworks and brass. Paul and his sister came to watch the fireworks from Holzli's house since it was up so far on the hillside. Holzli's mother made them peanut butter sandwiches, which she should have known they hated because Holzli had told her.

The experiment had already been tried. Paul had told Holzli later that Elspet planned never to visit again. "She says, 'One never knows what one might be required to eat.'" But Paul had not looked happy himself, laboring conscien-tiously to get his own sandwich down. They both endured the present trial, too, lubricated with *Apfelsaft,* though the girl's face was a theater of disgust and betrayal.

The three walked down to the village center afterwards, delaying in a meadow by the road to monitor an *Igel* waddling on some nocturnal expedition. The band music started before they got down, oompahs resounding between the walls of the closely packed houses near the bottom.

"They will walk from place to place, later," said Paul. "But, now, they are sitting in the courtyard by the church."

The musicians were in costume, all men, and Holzli knew some by sight. Scanning the ranks, he found the postmaster in the second row with one of the two flugelhorns. At least one too many, he thought. He watched him play until his eyes wandered to the other man and winter was on him again.

Herr Ehrlich met his stare without expression, blowing into his horn and working the valves. He seemed to need no help from the score in the little stand perched on his instrument. The boy glanced away for as long as he could and then back, and the teacher's attention—relentless, grey, unblinking—had not shifted from him.

"I must go," he said to Paul. "I am a little ill. I think it is the peanut butter."

"It does not matter so much. The music will all be very much the same. You will not miss anything. It is a shame you are not feeling well, though."

"I am not surprised at all," Elspet commented just loudly enough for him to hear.

Summer had brought a green to the hills and fields so intense and pervasive it made the land look artificial. The slant of the light at day's beginning or end heightened the effect. In the August sunrise, from his post above the house, he could have been looking at a carpeted surface. It must once have been all forest, he suspected, pushed up through centuries to the summits.

But, it was certainly not all cultivated and, even up among the trees, one found meadows that had never endured a plow. Had it all been grazed, at one time or another? Where he lived was called *Im Hengsten*—among the stallions— despite there being no evidence of horses. Whatever the case, the valley seemed like a golf-course or a park, broken to human will and comfort. It made him feel at peace and trapped.

Nothing more would happen until September, and he slept and woke when he wanted, again. Sunday, he was rousted early, but he made it up later in the day. He knew there would be a reckoning, when the summer finally ended and he had to readjust to the cadence of the school. There was nothing to be done about it, however—he would simply have to go sleepless to Zürich that first day. That was a future day; he did not have to worry about it now.

The twenty-four hour cycle that ruled the world did not rule him. His day was longer, for some reason. An extraterrestrial provenance? Another planet with a slower rotation and a superior culture? Perhaps. All he really knew was that he hated to go to sleep before exhaustion forced him. It brought a final end to things, and he did not want to go earlier than he had to. Not that being awake was all that great, he considered.

By the end of the night, he was close enough to sleep that the great, green vista was even less natural. More deliberate. Something could be found if he looked hard enough, if he went far enough over the hills and out of sight beyond them. He was always too tired actually to go, and, later in the day, after he had slept, the promise was no longer there.

The last night came, a Sunday, and he could not sleep. That morning, they had gone into the city as usual. It was a sort of trial run for the days ahead—the church was not far from the school, close to the consulate. He tried to stay awake the rest of the day. Their weekly promenade helped, but his body betrayed him before the afternoon was out. Awakened for dinner, he had slept long enough to keep him going, wide-eyed and alert, into the morning hours.

He was not in the middle of a book and had none to start. His old materials from the international school were still where had had set them almost three months before, whitened now with dust. He could not look through them; he would be immersed in their like soon enough. He passed, by association, to the village things. Again, he pulled out the notebook from religion class.

For the Ninth Commandment, he had copied a diagram of a situation where one might be tempted to bear false witness but should not. Two witnesses named W and F stood side by side in the street. An Automobilist, labeled A, was driving down the street, sensibly straight and steady to judge from his arrow. A *Velo* driver, a bicyclist, O, had apparently, for no sane reason, looped in and out of side streets and around buildings and into the path of the car.

The collision produced a yellow cloud or, perhaps, a fire. Holzli did not think it was a separate thing they were both running into—a bush, say—because it had no identifying letter. Why W and F would bear false witness was not clear, but since they and O were all circles and A was a rectangle, prejudice might be suggested. Holzli did not remember. The buildings were elaborate; one seemed to have a skylight.

He turned on the radio, but the first song played was "Homeward Bound," which had run through his head the whole week of *Pfadfinder* camp. It saddened him, and he twisted the dial off again.

Sleep kept its distance. The desk also held one of the new Superballs they had invented in the States and a piece of leather equipped with fur and eyes, which arched its back when you petted it. There was also an old *Classics Illustrated* that had been with him since New Jersey. It was their version of Caesar's *Gallic War,* and Holzli had searched it out again to read, a few weeks before, because he remembered it had Helvetii in it, being conquered.

Switzerland dubbed itself Helvetia on its coins. He guessed that was fair. He thought of the Swiss as Teutonic infantrymen; if the comic book was right, they started as Celts, but at least they were not pictured with cavalry. That would have been too hard to swallow—he just did not associate this folk with horses, despite his house's place name. The only horses he knew outside Einsiedeln were on the other side of the valley, and there were not many of them.

His Swiss-Italian friend with the Winnetou movies lived near the stables. Earlier that summer, the boy's parents had decided he should learn to ride, and they negotiated a group price for lessons from the horses' owner. They talked Holzli and his parents into joining in and sharing the cost along with two German girls who lived in the village but whom

Holzli had never met. He never did meet them—his friend found out he would not be learning Western saddle and refused to go through with the deal.

It did not matter now. School was starting and the months of peace and freedom were over.

He slept again, finally, two hours before he had to get up. The alarm pulled him up from deep below the surface and deposited him on his feet, conscious but not happy about it. He could barely think—scarcely act—and he did not trust his stomach enough to eat. Dressing took all the time he had before leaving the house.

He did not have new books yet, but he managed to remember to fill the attaché case with pens and notebooks. As he turned to close his door, he saw his old football on the floor beneath his dresser and, only dimly intending anything, moving as if forcing his way through glycerin, he retrieved it. It was too big for the case, although it had lost air, and he did not want to carry it in public, so he went up to the kitchen and got a paper bag.

The ball was close to official size. Holzli's hands were big, his fingers long, and he could almost handle a full-size ball. He thought his hands looked like the skeletons of bat wings, though the last piano teacher he had before he quit, Herr Baumann, had prized them. "Your fingers were made for this—they are gifts. Or, they would be if you had any especial talent."

He had never been outstandingly good as a quarterback either, but he could hold on to the ball and could often put it where it was supposed to go. It did not matter what position he played, really; he was bringing the ball mostly, he decided, because no one else might have thought of it. Bagged, it could pass for a lunch if he judged it should not come out.

Lunch! He had forgotten. Sawing off a quarter of a loaf of bread, he put it in his case and forced the lid shut, waved and grunted to his parents, who were fixing breakfasts, and hurried down the stairs and out the door.

Mr. Reilly was their main teacher again. Mr. Hughes had left the country for another job, and they wanted to start the woman who replaced him with a lower grade. The class moved to the seventh-grade classroom, next door to the old room, but that was the only change.

He had gained clarity and energy by the time he reached the city, and he still felt almost normal at noon. It was his first chance to talk to Konrad, who had come late. They met in the garden and said hello, then sat and ate and fed crumbs to the sparrows that landed around their feet. When Mark came up, Konrad remembered something he needed to find in the library, and Holzli went back up to the classroom.

The permanent pitcher was there, talking to a new blonde from Michigan. Holzli shifted through the books stacked along the window at the front of the room. When a group of kids came in, the new girl was drawn away. Holzli hesitated for a moment, then went over to the pitcher.

"I brought a football."

The boy looked at him but did not open his mouth. Debby Petersen, however, who had come in with the others, snatched the occasion, raptor-like. "We don't *play* football. We play *baseball*." The boy smiled blandly at him, then, still unspeaking.

Holzli looked away, but everywhere he turned his head, he met another face with the same muted smile, except on Debby, who smirked openly. He turned back and dropped his eyes, and they fell on the boy's pink hands and stubby fingers.

CHAPTER 24

The late November wind insinuated itself into the mansion. No one knew where it found entrance. All doors and windows were sound, and the classrooms were warm enough when everything was shut. Still, the open cavern beneath the dome made up half of the building; any breeze that made its way inside could go anywhere left unguarded.

Outside, the city was having a season of grace—the snow had melted and was not yet replaced. The wind used the opportunity to hunt out all the leaves that remained on the walks and streets, and set them swirling away. One could hear it trying to get through the windows into the classroom. The pipes and radiator clanked and pinged and hissed loudly enough to drown it out, sometimes, yet the sound was always there underneath.

The radiator also made it hard to hear Mr. Reilly from where Holzli sat near the back. He glared over at it and noticed Mark's desk was still empty. Mark had asked permission to use the lavatory, but that must have been twenty minutes ago.

Holzli looked back to the front and saw that Mr. Reilly had been watching him. The teacher seemed just as puzzled as he, however, and when he had finished marking the meter on the line he was scanning, he said, "Lloyd! Go see what's keeping your friend Buzzell!"

The lavatories were on the second floor. The boy sprinted down the steps with his hand sliding on the banister for balance, trying to do this as quickly as he could so Mark would not cost him more class time than necessary. The last time he had been sent from the room on an errand, Mr. Reilly said things that ended up on the test. And to call Mark his friend, in front of everyone! He supposed it was true, but it was nothing one wanted highlighted.

No one was in the lavatory. After banging the door noisily open and calling Mark's name, Holzli investigated the three stalls. When he returned to the classroom and shrugged at Mr. Reilly, the teacher broke off in the middle of whatever point he was making. He strode through the desks to the door, pausing to hook his fingers into Holzli's left biceps and drag him along. He closed the door behind them. His hold was strong enough to hurt; the student could tell it was an indulgence having little to do with the present situation.

"You didn't find him?"

"He wasn't in the bathroom."

"You three are always playing the fool, and I'm becoming very, very tired of it. I won't put up with it forever."

This struck Holzli like a physical blow—he had had no idea Mr. Reilly disliked him so vehemently. He was not quite sure the teacher was talking sense. At any rate, he could not think of much any of them had done worth this rancor.

"Go in and get Müller and meet me in the Headmaster's rooms," the Irishman said, releasing his grip, finally.

Holzli rubbed his arm, feeling for puncture wounds.

Mark was not in the building. They had searched with the help of Frau Geiger and Mr. Austin's secretary while the seventh grade was set to doing a pop trig quiz. Now, they were combing the neighborhood while the secretary tried to reach the missing boy's parents.

For his part, Holzli chose the lakeshore, where he would only have to scan one direction for Mark's short, dark-headed form. He went north a bit, for completeness' sake, but then turned south and walked on, till he came to the limnigraph at the water's edge opposite the park. He missed the swans and ducks that would have followed him like a destroyer escort in warmer times. A voice reached him from the distance. He could not tell who was called, so he merely bent his path slightly toward the park and kept going.

The wind had kept itself in check; it rushed back suddenly and forcefully a soon as he left the big elms behind, hitting him head-on at first, then churning the world around him. Something got in his eye, and he ran back to the protection of the biggest tree—the one that backed home plate.

He had always been fond of this particular tree. Somehow, admiration had grown into affection. Elms rarely attained much size, he had been told, but this one was a meter and a half in diameter. Its neighbors were oversized too—one had branched into two trunks that threatened to pull apart from their own bulk—but it had no pressing rivals. Presumably, it was ages old; vines covered it so continuously and thickly they were like a second bark.

The voice faded in and out as the wind shifted. It was closer than it had been and carried urgency. He was too intent on getting the speck out of his eye to look for the source of the call.

"Holzli!" he heard clearly by the time his eye was clear. Now, he saw Konrad running toward him, his mouth opened greedily for air. "Holzli! Come back in! They have found him!"

The two walked back slowly when the German boy's breathing was gentle enough for speech. "Frau Geiger saw him coming down the walk, headed back to the school. He was talking to himself very loudly and did not pay Frau Geiger much attention at first when he came to her. Mr. Austin and his wife have him in the office. Reilly went up to class, and we are supposed to go back there."

The secretary was watching for them, however, and caught them as they came in. "The Headmaster would like to see the both of you after school if that is possible."

"How is Mark?" Holzli asked her.

"I do not know," she answered. "They are still talking to him. If the Headmaster wishes to tell you anything when you come by, you can find out then."

"Buzzell has already gone home. His mother was able to come and take him."

Mrs. Austin had hurried out, with a nod, as they entered. Her husband seated them in old, mismatched armchairs he kept in his inner office for visitors. He sat in the chair to his desk, turned around to face them across a table swarming with books and the vestiges of tea.

"I just put the water on again if you would like tea. No more biscuits, I'm afraid."

He stared up at the ceiling to his right long enough for Holzli to get curious and turn to look. Nothing was there that he could see, but, as soon as he faced away, the Headmaster spoke again. "We have instant coffee, too."

Holzli declined both, but Konrad, as always, wanted coffee and loaded the cup half full with milk, trying to approximate the *Milchkaffee* he drank at every opportunity.

"I'm having you two in because I'm told you're Buzzell's closest friends."

Neither made any response, but the man seemed to be speaking from some other place where he could not really see them, anyway.

"He was acting very oddly when he returned to us. Mrs. Geiger says he was having one side of a conversation with himself. Very...absorbedly."

Though Mr. Austin was not smoking at the moment, the atmosphere in the room was hazy. The titles of books on farther shelves were hard to read. Holzli ordinarily liked tobacco smoke, and he planned to have cigarettes specially made for himself from a mixture of Balkan and Turkish tobaccos when he was old enough. Right now, however, breathing this, he felt a slender sharpness behind his eye. Soon, everything might be lined with light.

"Does...well...have either of you ever felt that your friend was experiencing...difficulties?"

"What do you mean?" asked Konrad.

The Headmaster became preoccupied with the ceiling again. "Has he ever appeared other than...conventional...in his thinking?"

With a thoughtful expression, Konrad answered, "No," and the other boy echoed him, trying to look puzzled at the very question.

"I see. Then, I'll ask another question. This is not on my own initiative, you understand. I don't imagine there is any substance to this particular concern. His parents think it's important I ask, however."

The boys stole glances at one another and waited.

"I'm aware these things go on, of course. I, myself, had a passing acquaintance with hashish in North Africa during the War." He regarded Konrad for a moment. "Remarkable, your Rommel."

He was silent then, until Holzli began to fear he would vanish into reverie altogether and said, "Mark doesn't use dope. None of the kids do."

"No one has been able to find out where to get it," Konrad volunteered.

"I didn't think so," Mr. Austin said. "Good, good. Well, he should be back in class with you soon, as far as I know. Should you find out anything from him that might be helpful, we would all be appreciative. Look after him."

Outside, Holzli worked his lungs like bellows, hoping it was not too late to avert the headache.

He made it to the platform in the Bahnhof before he had to give up hope. As he watched the train come toward him down the track, the lights on its green engine suddenly flared, and he knew he had not escaped.

The evening was a waste, and he awoke the next morning with no schoolwork done. His parents would not let him stay home—they were convinced that honest explanations would excuse him. He could not tell them he had used the same story too often before.

Mark, on the other hand, missed that day and the next. The day he reemerged, he was granted a strange deference by everyone, child and adult. No one, of course, showed any active kindness—nature would not bend so far—but he was honored with neglect.

Holzli and Konrad themselves were not sure how to approach him. They let the lunch hour pass without speaking to him, and he showed no interest in them. Konrad's patience, though, could not survive the afternoon. At break, he followed Mark to a bench among the bushes that held the park on the farthest side.

Holzli almost let him go alone, afraid of crowding Mark. It was too much to ask of himself, though. Konrad must have something in mind, well thought out or not. If he got Mark to talk, Holzli wanted to hear. He waited until the blond boy was halfway across the grass, then started to follow, slowly, in his turn.

By the time he came to the bench, his eyes on the pair ahead of him the whole while, it was clear Konrad still had no notion what to say. The one boy sat and gazed off into the sky that streamed grey above the ballplayers' heads. The other stood slightly to his front, in sight if Mark chose to see him.

"Konrad! Mark! What are you guys doing?" Holzli attempted. It did not work. The sitting figure might have been sculptured, voiceless and immobile.

"Mark," said Konrad, then. "What happened to you? Why did you wander off from school?"

At last, Mark's vision dropped to take them in. "You said you didn't want to hear any more about it."

"So, then, this is still your back-in-time story".

"Yeah. Since you don't want to hear about it, you should both go away and not bother me."

Holzli looked to Konrad for confirmation as he said, "We don't think you're just lying, anymore. We think you may be nuts. So does Mr. Austin, I think,"

Konrad nodded.

Mark smiled a fragile smile. "So do my parents."

"But you probably don't think so."

"I know what I see and hear."

"Okay," took up Konrad. "What, therefore, did you see and hear that led you away from literature class?"

"Nothing. I had to go to the bathroom. *Then* I saw something."

"What did you see in the bathroom?"

"Not *in* the bath room. On the way there. On the stairs."

Both listeners had come closer and were now standing over Mark, so he stood up, too, and stepped back to put space between them.

"I had passed the third floor and was going around the next bend. I was going pretty fast, so I was looking down to watch my step. As I rounded the bend, though, I looked up and saw that I was about to run into this girl.

"I thought she was a nun, at first, from the way she was dressed. She would have looked about like a high school girl except for the clothes. And something about her face—*in* her face—seemed too grown up. Too tired, maybe. You could see that, even though she had a real shocked look, too. Then, I thought she might be one of those teachers who come to sit in on classes before they're hired."

"Because they hire a lot of nuns here," commented Holzli.

"Hey! I was just trying to figure out why this person might be standing there. Anyway, she wasn't a nun. I just didn't expect to see that kind of clothes nowadays.

"I stopped because she seemed so scared I was going to run her down, but her mouth and eyes stayed wide open even after I stopped. I stared at her and things started clicking. First, I recognized those clothes, and that made me really look at her face and, all of a sudden, I knew who she was. She was taller and older and prettier, but it was Regula."

CHAPTER 25

Mark paused. 'I'm not going to have time to tell all of this."

"We would like to hear whatever you have time for," Konrad assured him.

"Then, you are, really, willing to listen to this?"

"Yes, we told you that."

"But the gist of it," said Holzli, "is that you were wandering around talking to Regula all the time you were gone."

"Did she recognize you without being told?" Konrad asked.

"Let me do this my own way or it's going to get all screwed up. Yes, she did recognize me because I hadn't changed any. It hasn't been very long for me. For her, it was three years.

"'But, you have not changed at all,' she said to me. 'Is it because our times have been different again?'

"I said yes, because that was obviously what happened, but it didn't explain anything.

"Her voice had changed, too. It's all low and smooth now, and sort of purry."

"Purry? She sounds like a happy cat?" Holzli immediately regretted the interruption, but, for him, at least, Mark was rapidly losing the sacrosanctity with which he had returned to school that morning.

"No! I just don't know how to say what she sounds like. Never mind. She sounds different from how she sounded before.

"Anyway, I was the *only* thing she recognized. She was shocked by suddenly finding herself with me on the stairs in a weird building, but she wasn't really that scared. She thought she was dreaming because she came there from a dream."

"What..." Konrad started and stopped.

"I mean, she had been asleep. In her sleep, some sort of person came to her and told her she could be free if she could find me."

They waited with controlled expressions.

"She didn't know how she found me—she spent a lot of time searching in some way she really didn't understand herself. She said it was like groping around for something half-asleep in the dark. Of course, she was totally asleep, but that's what she said it was like.

"Finally, she found me and, then, she was on the steps. It took a long time to talk her into believing it was real."

"I asked her what she was supposed to be free from. She told me what happened since the last time we saw each other. Her father came back for them—her stepfather, the one who escaped from prison. They left Zürich and went north across the Rhine. They spent the next three years moving around in some place called...Swabia?"

Holzli shrugged.

"It is the region north of here, across the Rhine," Konrad informed them.

"'We could have been safe there,' she said. 'Not every place cared what people believed as long as they did not cause trouble. My father, however, must always be trying to make converts. And he is right—survival is not the important thing.

"'Some places are Reformer and some are Catholic, but they are all afraid of Baptizers who try to recruit others. It is because of when the peasants revolted—the princes think Baptizers led that. There is still a special corps of a thousand men who hunt us down and can kill us where they find us, without trial. If we stayed quiet in the land, we would be safe, but we cannot.'

"'Why do they think Baptizers led the peasants?' I asked.

"'Perhaps some did—or some who called themselves by that name. But none who take the sword can claim that name now. The meeting at Schleitheim settled that for once and all about the time we left Zürich.'

"I didn't ask her to go into that. I did ask her again what she wanted to be free from.

"'My father has been arrested at last. The church where we live now has made the magistrate move against him. He will certainly be beheaded or burned. I expect they will come for my mother and me soon. Women they still drown.'

"'This person in your dream meant you could escape if you found me?' I asked. 'Am I supposed to help you somehow? What am I supposed to do?'

"'I do not know,' she said. 'I do not know that I want to escape, for that matter. Some times, when I think of death, I am so frightened I despair. Other times, however, the thought of giving my life in witness of my faith fills me with a burning joy. I could go to the stake myself and scarcely feel the flames by contrast. And, other times, I am simply at peace, willing to take whatever comes, death or life.

"'So, I do not know I would escape if that were offered me. I suppose, on balance, I would rather live than die, but by so fine a difference it is hardly important to me.

"'In all events, I am here with you for a time.' She looked around her, then worked up a smile. 'And where *is* here?'

"'You're back in Zürich.' It was the easiest thing to say because it didn't really tell her anything. I knew, though, that I'd have to come clean with her. I couldn't keep pretending I was from her time.

"'Look,' I said to her. 'I wasn't honest with you before. I'm not from Prague. I'm from here, and this is Zürich, but this isn't the 1500's.'

"She held onto her smile. 'I...I have already understood that. The way in which I had to search to find you let me know that. What age, then, is this? It is after my lifetime— that is clear to me.'

"'What can I tell her?' I wondered. I thought of all the stories I read where someone finds out something about the future and it changes everything. But, I didn't feel like lying to her anymore. Luckily, I didn't know much about things she'd be interested in. We figured that out pretty quickly.

"I didn't know anything at all about her or her family. I could tell her some things about the Reformation, but mostly that things turned into a big mess all over Europe. That didn't surprise her. Everything changed too much too fast after her time for her to care about them. Really, she was just sad because of that—the things she cared about got left behind.

"We went outside, and she could see how things had changed. Cars and stuff like that threw her, but not as much as I expected. It was still like she was in a dream and sort of...protected or far off."

"Buffered," Holzli suggested.

"Detached," said Konrad.

Mark gave no sign he heard either. "She was willing to believe that lots of new things were found out about after her time. Once she saw something like a car, she accepted it and let it drop. I think she could see she wouldn't understand much about how they worked and that it wasn't important.

"'It is like the new lands they found across the ocean,' she said. She'd been smiling a lot all this time, and she smiled again, then, like she was remembering something. 'When my father and the others escaped from the tower, one of the men wanted everyone to flee across the seas and live with the Red Indians.'"

"Well, these were all Germans, sort of," Holzli remarked. "That would have appealed to all of them."

Konrad was distracted—or pretended to be—by music from a car radio. The car was distant, only near enough to see the driver's window open even in this cold. The wind blew steady today. "Good Vibrations" came directly to them in the breeze.

"That will not last long," said Konrad. "The Swiss will get him for that—he and his car will vanish any second now as though they had never been."

"In the meantime, though," Holzli said, "that song's the best thing any band has done this year."

"Nonsense. 'Devil with a Blue Dress On' is better. You just like that electronic instrument because it is odd."

As Mark had told of Regula smiling under the caress of memory, he had smiled himself. Now, it looked as if he had lost the others' attention. He bobbled the smile for a moment and finally dropped it. "Do you want to hear any more of this?"

The testiness in his tone startled both into silence. He moved to fill the opening before it could close. "We were in the park by then. Over there." He waved toward the water. "'This is the lake,' she said. 'The same lake I could always see from home. I had not thought to see it again. How far are we from Zollikon?'

"I did not know how to answer. 'Too far to walk now. I can't be gone long. We can't go to the old part of the city, either. That's too bad—you could probably see familiar stuff. I don't think it can have changed much. We're about halfway between the old city and Zollikon, actually.'

"'Yes. This is the Horn. I recognize it now. It is a matter of filtering out the strange and discovering one's own things underneath.

"'I came along here on my way to the city many times. One time, however, I remember best of all.'

"She took my hand, then, and we walked like that, but it wasn't the way it was before. It was like a big sister holding your hand."

Holzli had not been looking at Mark. He was still facing the lake, watching the kids there in case they heard the bell and started to go in. When Mark had been quiet curiously long, however, he turned to him. Mark's chin was on his chest. The good eye was away from Holzli; the small muscles around the other barely ever moved, anyway—they gave away nothing. Only the effort Mark was making to keep his lips tight showed.

Konrad walked a few paces forward and stood with his back to them. "It is significant that the New World had just been discovered. They would not have had potatoes before that. They could not have made *Röschti*. We are observing the birth of Swiss national identity."

"Is it about time to go back?" Mark asked in a voice that trembled no more than usual.

"Not yet." Holzli resumed his guard on the ballplayers. "We may have a lot of time, yet. Go on with your story."

"It's not a story."

"Your report. Your...narration. Whatever."

There was no response.

"Well, I guess we can go in early."

"She said, 'It was in June of the year you and I first met. We were like an invading force descending down on Zürich from Zollikon. Every Baptizer I knew was with us, men, women and children. We wore ropes or willow twigs in place of girdles, as Isaiah says folk will at the Last Judgment. We were coming to pronounce judgment on the city.

"'The troop stopped here to rest. We were making slow time with all our very young and very old. Some brought out wine and bread or cheese, but my mother had carried barley porridge for my father and me in a little earthenware pot. She wanted me to collect wood to heat it.

"'There had been a grove of elm trees near where we sat, it appeared. Most were stumps, recently hewn, but around the survivors was a little thicket of saplings. I pulled on one of those, and it would not yield, so I started to tug it back and forth.

"'I must have looked like a dog worrying a rag. My mother saw and made me stop. Live wood would not burn, she said. I should hunt for pieces on the ground. It may have been too late for the little elm—leaves and twigs had been stripped off, leaving wounds.

"'We arrived in the afternoon and marched through the city, summoning the citizens to repentance and warning the stiff-necked of their coming destruction. Forty days, we said. Forty days and then the Judgment. Woe to Zürich! Woe! Woe!'

"Her smile was different. She had a big grin, now. 'Of course, forty days later, nothing happened. It was fun, though. We shouted that Pastor Zwingli was the dragon of the Apocalypse, persecuting the true Church. It did not make him like us, but nothing would, and it was the truth, in a way. By the end there was nothing but open truth to face him with. He was too complete a sophist, my father said, for reason to touch him. He had shown his skill in the debates. So we marched into the city and unmasked him and left.

"'No one paid attention, but one cannot take consequences as one's guide. We said what needed to be said. That was our victory.'

"'I don't understand,' I told her.

"'What do you not understand?'

"'What you said about consequences.'

"'I simply mean that you cannot ever know what will come of your actions so you cannot ever worry about what will happen. You can only do the right thing and leave the results to God.

"'My father says that is why violence is always wrong. You know you will hurt someone, but you cannot know that any good will come of it. It is best not even to act without violence unless you know your intentions are pure—that you are acting from love and not anger or pride. Anger and pride are sins for certain, and you can never know what your actions will lead to.'

"'You all believe that?'

"Her grin got bigger. 'My father is more extreme than most.

"'We do all agree, at least, that violence to defend yourself is wrong. You hurt your brother to no purpose. Nothing really bad can happen to one whose faith is firm. That is why I almost do not care whether I live or die.'"

"This is shit!" Konrad spat. "This is an argument for staying out of politics and letting the gangsters take over! She is a tool for that!"

"Hah! Then you think she's real!" said Holzli.

"No, I do not!" He rounded on Mark. "Did you ask her why she has a man's name?"

"Yes, I did. She said a lot of women were named Regula. She said it's a Latin word that means 'a rule,' and it's feminine in gender, so it works good for women. And she said that, back when she was still in Zürich, Zwingli's wife had a little girl, and they named her Regula. You can check on that, if you want."

"I do not want. And I have heard the bell. See, they are going in."

CHAPTER 26

The snow was returning. Holzli could smell it in the black morning even before the clouds could be seen. All day long, the lower air was still, though they could see the heavens rolling. All day long, at every moment, they expected the first flakes. When the school released them late that day, the walks were dry.

"So, you have talked with Mark some more," Konrad asserted.

"Yeah, during lunch yesterday. It's hard to catch him. He has someplace he disappears to during breaks. It's not any place easy to guess—I've looked."

Holzli started off, but the other stayed where he was beside the square stone pillars of the gate.

"What are you waiting for?" Holzli asked.

"My mother has gone to Berlin on business. My father and I are having dinner out. He is coming by to pick me up."

"I'll have to tell you tomorrow, then, the other stuff Mark said. If you're interested."

"Not really. Did he tell you what they did to him when they got him home?"

Cold tapped Holzli's ear. "Wait." He brushed it with his fingertips. It was wet. "Wait a minute."

Another flake hit his eyelid, then Konrad said, "Yes, I can feel it."

The snow that had held off since some time before dawn came now in a rush as though, having started, it could hold back nothing. Suddenly, it was evening, the farthest night had yet encroached upon the day. Looking down the lakeshore to the north, Holzli saw that falling flakes were sparkling in lights already lit in windows along the street. They looked like fireflies.

"I'd better get moving."

A car turned the corner down by the park. The engine sounded strangely close in the stillness that had dropped around them with the snow—a silence severe even for Zürich.

"This must be him. Wait, and we can see if he will give you a ride to the Bahnhof."

Holzli was not comfortable with the idea. He did not like asking for favors he did not actually need. His own father's dislike for the Müllers—for the son, at least, and almost certainly for the father—weighed on him as well. While he hesitated, though, the car pulled up before them.

He had met his friend's father several times in passing. An older, fleshier, darker Konrad with a close-cropped beard, Mr. Müller twisted across the seat to jerk the door open, then dropped back upright with a grunt Holzli could hear outside the car.

Konrad leaned in and traded words with his father. Withdrawing, he said, "Okay, get in the front," then squeezed his way into the back. As Holzli pulled the door shut behind himself and shifted into place, he saw the steering wheel and dashboard, and was smitten to the core of his being. The dash was like nothing he had seen in an automobile—it was the instrument panel for a jet or a spaceship. His seat, for that matter, was more aeronautic than automotive.

"Hello...Holzli, is it? How are you doing?"

"Fine."

"There is no problem with going by the train station. We are going to a restaurant close to there. We have not seen each other for a while."

"No." Holzli groped desperately for something to add. "What kind of car is this?"

"It is a Mercedes-Benz. A German car. Not like the cars you are used to, right?"

The boy had taken the Aston Martin DB series for his ideal till that evening. It was an abstract loyalty, however. He had never seen any of those in three dimensions; the Mercedes held the field through mere presence.

Still: "It's not a sports car, is it?"

"No, of course it is not a sports car." The car accelerated, as though challenged by the very question. "If we were on an open road, however, I could show you that that makes no difference. I have had this up to 193 kilometers per hour."

Mr. Müller turned at the next side street, not quite cornering well enough to stay out of the wrong lane. The boy could not tell if the fault lay with the machine or its driver. He suspected the latter. They were leaving their most direct route, and that seemed to be spontaneous whim.

"I tell you what. You live out in the country? Come dine with us, and I will drive you home afterwards. You will see what this pachyderm can be made to do."

He was sorry he had said anything. It was decided he would call his parents from the restaurant itself. The owner was a friend of Konrad's father, an expatriate Hessian, and Holzli was led into a backroom to use the telephone. He feared they all would stay and listen. His parents could not be told with whom he was eating, and he did not want to explain a lie to the Müllers. Luckily, the host took the pair out to select a table, and Holzli was left free to invent another family to feed him and bring him homeward through the storm.

Coming back into the dining room, he found Konrad trying to describe Mark's latest vagary. The father pushed a basket of rolls toward him, and the son said, "You talked with him more than I did. What else did he say?"

Holzli tore a piece from a roll and buttered it. He had picked this up in the Hotel Bahnhof—preparing and eating an entire half a roll (or a whole slice of bread) identified one as American.

"One thing was that his parents said if he kept acting like he was crazy, he was going to be sent back to Michigan and have to see psychiatrists. He's got an aunt he doesn't get along with who lives there. He'd have to live with her and go to public school."

Konrad's father snorted the way his son did when he was being superior.

"They would send him away from here for psychiatric treatment? From Zürich? That is not quite sane itself."

Holzli shrugged. "I just know what Mark told me," he mumbled around another bit of roll.

Wine arrived and Mr. Müller filled the boys' glasses without asking. Holzli had come to like the taste but could not accept it as a proper beverage. He thought it a cheat, promising to allay thirst but only increasing it. It was too late, however, to order the mineral water he could usually get away with.

"My son does not like wine," said Mr. Müller. "He says it gives him headaches, but it is because he would rather have *Milchkaffee*. He likes dairy products—he would have *Schlag* on everything if it were allowed him. Watch during dessert. By the time he goes to university, he will be obese."

"No, I like coffee because it stops the headaches."

"That is nonsense. I know of no authority who has made that connection."

This was a facet of his friend Holzli had never had reason to suspect. He would question him later, though—this looked like too miry a ground to accompany them onto.

He waited out the others' silence until he felt the topic had lapsed, then said "Mark also went into more about what the girl said her father believed."

"Konrad has been telling me about that. This was in a similar vein?"

"Sort of. Mark thinks it goes farther than what Konrad knows about. Something about trying to do something big usually causing the opposite to happen even if you don't use

-168-

force. Mark didn't understand why." He pretended to take a gulp of the wine, drawing only enough to wet his palate. "I've read something like that—it..."

"It is not worth a waste of your regard. Your friend's parents are undoubtedly right—he is dreadfully delusional. I would even say that, if he has further episodes of this sort, you have a moral obligation to let his family know. For his own sake." The elder Müller pulled down an unfeigned draught of wine. "His mother and father do know the full story, do they not?"

"Yes," the two boys lied in unison.

"If they do not, you are bound to tell them that, also."

Now, the food came, although Holzli had been expecting menus. They were all having chicken in some yellow sauce that was unfamiliar.

"You do not eat like an American," the father said, watching him. "You do not cut everything up and then transfer the fork to your other hand."

"This way made more sense once I saw people doing it, so I copied them. I can't do it around my parents. I tried and got yelled at."

"What is this name Holzli? It sounds like something your oath-comrades would come up with." He was translating the word *Eidgenossen,* Holzli knew—another thing the Swiss called themselves. "Schwyzerdütsch always tries to sound cute."

"Actually, I made it up. It's supposed to mean 'Woody,' my real name, which I don't like."

"Why not adopt a proper name?"

"How? I can get myself called by a nickname, but I can't just decide that I'm going to be 'James' or something."

Konrad began to spasm with soundless laughter. "Holzli likes spy movies," he explained when he was able.

"Excellent!" said his father, oddly and too loudly. The low murmur from the other tables broke off and resumed in an instant's time. Mr. Müller's skin was blushing red, Holzli noticed, deep enough to see in the restaurant's feeble light.

"I have something, then, that you would like to see. I have a Walther PPK at home."

Konrad smiled and nodded when the other boy turned to him.

The adult glanced ostentatiously around and curbed his voice. "The bloody Swiss must not know, of course. I only keep it as part of a small collection. I am a campaigner for pacifism, after all. I like the Walther for aesthetic reasons. It has an elegance of design, a crafted charm, as the Pistole 08 does—the Luger. You will have to come visit us in Zumikon and see."

"Drink!" he added, flicking Holzli's glass with his finger. It rang dully—it was nearly full. "You Americans are trained to fear alcohol. Even those who drink much feel guilt over it."

Lifting his own glass, half emptied, Konrad said, "Even Mark's Anabaptists enjoyed wine, if you remember that part of the story."

His father ate quickly and, waiting for them, lit a cigarette. He held it in his fingertips, almost like a pencil. Smoke ran slowly from his nostrils while he contemplated the glimmering ash.

"*That's* one thing Mark's people weren't doing," said Holzli.

"Oh, but it would barely have been discovered. I am sure that every *Wiedertaüfer* man in Europe owned a pipe as soon as tobacco became popular. It would have been very strange if they did not. They would have had no moral objection to it."

He was distressingly loud, again, and the boys' eyes flittered around, skimming the other diners.

"That and the hysteria about alcohol are purely American phenomena. Granted, the sickness has its roots hereabouts, with these Reformers. More with the Genevan genus, actually, I suppose. But it does not become truly pathological until it jumps the Atlantic."

He set the cigarette in a groove in the corner of a square, glass ashtray, but he misjudged the balance and it rolled onto the tablecloth. Snatching it up, he dropped it in the middle of the ashtray. The coal had broken off, and it took him three swipes with his hand to rake it onto the floor. He rubbed the black spot it left with his thumb, trying to see if the cloth was burned.

"Anyway," he said, picking up the pack and tapping out two more, "you need to do this once. Konrad does not get one. He steals enough of them from my cabinet."

"I do not. They cause headaches and force me to drink coffee. Do not do it, Holzli."

The American was not passing up the chance. He accepted his cigarette and Mr. Müller lit both.

"Breath it in—do not merely draw it into your mouth. That is how one smokes a pipe or cigar. This is different."

When Holzli had finished coughing and refused another trial, the man took the cigarette back and crushed it out in the ashtray. "So, you know that, now, at least, and can choose."

"Tschüss!" Konrad's father called to the owner and their waiter as they were leaving. The owner responded in kind. The waiter waved weakly and said nothing.

"What did they say?" Holzli asked his friend.

"It is how one says goodbye in Germany. Not here—but my father says it to the Swiss, too, to be annoying. He will not say 'adieu' to them. It is degenerate, he thinks. They are degenerate for saying it, he thinks. I do not know what they think of him, but many will not reply at all."

The driver seemed not to hear that the car had started and ground the ignition to convince himself. And then they were off. The snow had stopped while they were in the restaurant, and traffic had already cleared much of what had fallen on the roads. Holzli worried about ice, but the Mercedes gained speed with every stop sign and traffic light they ignored. It was late and dark and cold, and only a few were out to witness and wag their fingers.

When Holzli turned in his seat from time to time to take a reading of Konrad behind him, he saw resigned apathy. Mr. Müller himself had exhausted his dinnertime volubility—he was mute except to ask directions once they abandoned the Limmat for the hills and bends that would take them to the village. Those did not slow him.

Holzli could barely sense the tires slip on the curves, but it scared him. He could not see the point in going this fast unless the driver was trying to beat his own record. In the very second he squinted toward the speedometer, a siren started to heehaw, and the car's deceleration bounced him against the dash.

A red light pulsed in the mist behind. As the Mercedes slowed further, a police car came into focus and hung on their tail, not attempting to pass. *"Na also,* they are after us," Konrad's father rumbled. "Bloody Swiss bastards."

He stamped on the accelerator as if squashing an insect. Holzli, still perching forward in his seat, was yanked in the other direction and pressed into the cushions. The tires gripped hardly at all, however. Their car rotated out of their lane, forcing the police to leave the road altogether. Holzli had time to think how rarely he heard a siren like that outside of movies, and then a tree stopped their spin, striking a fender and leaving the two cars facing each other across the road like combatants, headlight to headlight.

"They have taken his driver's license. We will not be able to drive you home. I do not know yet how we will get back to Zumikon."

The two boys stood together at the edge of the road. The flasher continued to throw its light out into the air, catching the flakes of the returning snow so that they flared red like volcanic fire falling upon the men and vehicles.

"Their station has called your parents to pick you up. I do not imagine, from what you have said, that your parents would help us get to the train."

It shamed and saddened Holzli as much as anything ever had to nod agreement.

Across the road, on the far side of the Mercedes, two tiny circles lit up beneath the lowest branches of the trees. Holzli stared at them until they disappeared with a movement of the undergrowth only just visible at the limit of the light. It was too big to be a cat, too furtive to be a dog.

If he had not been embarrassed to face his friend, he would have missed the eyes when they reappeared a little to the right of their first position. Slowly, his own footsteps muffled for him in the carpeted valley, he crossed the road.

Deafened and intent, he never heard the car as it rounded the bend twenty meters down and sped toward him.

What registered with him was the tackle that carried him out of the lane and slammed him to the ground. Now, he heard the car squeal as, with better luck than the Müllers' car, it lost and regained traction, and braked to a stop.

The new driver ran back to them. Seeing Konrad's father and the boy stand up with no apparent injuries, he shifted his attention to the officers, shouting his defense to them as he came.

Soon, yet another automobile arrived, the Lloyds' Volkswagen. The two fathers avoided looking at each other the entire time it took for identifications to be made and explanations given. As he was driven away into the storm, Holzli looked back to where the shining circles still watched from the woods.

His father had added the *Tageblatt* to the *Herald Tribune* as daily reading. He translated an editorial aloud, a grievance against foreign drivers. "'They claim, always, that they will reform. But will they ever?'"

He looked over at his son. "Let me be perfectly unambiguous this time: you are not to associate with the Müller boy again. You have to be in the same classroom—let that be the fullest extent of your relations."

CHAPTER 27

The sun followed its spiraling path farther down the sky with each new day, leaving the northern world prey to the ice and darkness that had been waiting their opportunity. At last, the sky itself frosted over, sealing in the cold.

Sometimes even yet, however, the atmosphere would clear, and the moon and stars show through. They were there, above, by pure and happy chance, on the night of the last *Pfadfinder* campout of the year. The boys were not allowed to sleep beneath them, in the open, because of the temperature, but they sat outside, warmed by the fire, until the wood burned out.

One of the scouts, Thomas, whose *Pfadi* name was Tintin, had walked out into the night to relieve himself long enough before that it was growing strange. They began to shout his name, but nothing came back to them.

"*Ohren wie ein Hase,*" Holzli thought it safe to joke, since no one seemed genuinely worried as yet. Ears like a hare, he was trying to say. They all laughed, though he was never confident that they ever laughed entirely with him.

"*Ohren wie ein Hase,*" several called to Tintin when he finally stumbled from the woods.

"What is that supposed to mean?"

"It is what Holzli said about you."

Holzli felt bad, then, whether the joke had succeeded or not. He liked Tintin, who had recently developed a taste for translations of Mark Twain and liked to talk about them.

"The school in this *Tom Sawyer* is just like ours," he had decided, and Holzli was not moved to disagree.

There was nothing to be done—Tintin would either take the joke in good humor or not. Holzli was not sure, now, how he himself had intended it, and that troubled him. He shrugged at Tintin, who sat down on the other side of the fire, his face distorted beyond deciphering by the flicker of flame and shadow.

"What were you doing out there?" someone asked.

"That is no concern of yours," Tintin said. "But, also, I was looking up. We have not had the heavens so bright for a long time."

They all looked up, then, and no one spoke again until a voice whispered, "That must be Saturn there near the moon."

"And that is Jupiter to the east," said another.

A point of light began to cross the sky, a coursing star against the fixed.

"That must be one of yours. You, Holzli. Perhaps a Gemini. You have been missing Herr Lehrer Ehrlich's lectures."

"I do not think any Gemini's are up this month," Holzli said. "I think that is Swiss."

There was general laughter, but a different voice, which the American took for Tintin's, protested, "We could build one if we wanted—if there were some point to it."

"It cannot be that difficult," said someone else. Identities were blurring for Holzli in the dancing dark.

"But it costs a lot of money."

"Only if one wishes to send people up. There have been rockets for a long time now. It cannot be very expensive anymore."

"Is that true, Holzli? How much does it cost your country to send a rocket up?"

Could it be very much? Holzli had no basis for judgment, but he tried to imagine what was needed. If all you wanted was to put something into space—or even high enough to impress—not much could be required. A hull of some sort with a nosecone and fins, and some kind of fuel. Tin cans and gunpowder.

The instant he pictured it, he was enraptured. To be able to send something so far it left boundaries behind altogether was nearly to go yourself. And perhaps a step toward that. "I do not know, but it cannot be much. We could build one."

"Do you know how?"

"Of course. It is simple. We just need..." He stopped himself. He had been about to list the first things that came into his mind: tin cans, a funnel, and a mound of brass caps from *Fasnacht* guns. Just in time, though, the limits of his knowledge closed in on him—there was one big thing he did not understand. It would take research. "We need money."

"You can pay for it. You are rich."

"All Americans are rich."

"I am not. My family gives me nothing. We must all give money for this."

In the tent, later, he dreamt of a rocket up beyond the air, spraying fire from its tail to push against...nothing. It stayed there for a moment, in place, like a cartoon character who has run off a cliff but not yet looked down. Then the rocket fell, back into the clouds below and through them to the earth.

"Wake up!"

He tried to sit up, only distantly awake, and struggled in the confinement of the sleeping bag.

"What? What?" he slurred in English.

"You were having a dream," someone said.

"Yes," Tintin concurred. "You were saying, 'Oh. Raquel, Raquel! My dear!'" This last was in English, in the exaggerated Jersey accent they used to make fun of him.

"I do not think so. But, sorry."

When everyone had settled back again, he worked his arm out and felt the pack next to his head where he had put the thirty-two *Franken* he collected in donations. He did not need to check, he knew. The pack could have been left outside on the ground all night, and the money would still have been there in the morning. Still, old instincts died hard and slowly.

They had Mass late in the morning, under a sky that closed up on them just as they finished. The tents were down, the fires dead beyond resurrection, and everyone safely out of the hills before the snow could catch them.

Holzli climbed up the other side of the valley and came home to discover a strange car on the shoulder of the road in front. He stopped to drop his pack and Mountie hat on his bed and continued on up to where the Adlers sat with his mother at the dining room table.

"Niels brought the chessboard," his father said, walking in from the living room with a drink in each hand.

"And I have been waiting to put it to use," the Dane said. "Sit here. I have hardly seen you for months and months."

They did not talk, however. Mr. Adler kept a place in the adult conversation throughout the game, right up to the point at which he said, "Another two moves, and I will have your other rook. After that, you are quickly lost."

He did not give advice, nor did he offer the move back. "You do not have a board, am I right? Let me leave this one here, and you can play with situations on your own. I can give you books, if I remember to, that set out problems."

Holzli grunted to show he heard, but he was not going to concede purely on trust. While drinks and topics shifted and renewed around him, he sat unmoving, glaring at the board.

"I have only seen you a couple of times since your trip to Einsiedeln. How did that go?"

"Okay," said Holzli, but that seemed too curt for courtesy's sake, and he added, "I enjoyed it. I didn't expect anything like that in Switzerland." His eye stayed clamped to their object.

"Why?"

The boy reflected. "It's too Catholic. It's too fancy. I went in one Catholic church in Zürich that didn't even have a crucifix, like they were afraid of what the Reformers would think. This had all those altars."

"Which altars did you look at?"

"All of them. Well, I spent the most time at St. Maurice."

"Why? And give up on the game—we can start another."

"I don't know. It turned out, though, that he's important for Zürich. Their patron saints were soldiers of his."

"Yes. Very good. But, you do not know, then, that he was important here, also."

"Here? This village?"

"This canton. The whole canton was once traded for St. Maurice's lance."

"Set the pieces up again. I give up."

"Woody, you set them up if you want to play," his father told him. The grown-ups' talk had faded as the two conversed. "Don't speak to adults like that."

"It is all right," said Mr. Adler.

"Does anyone need refreshing?" Holzli's mother asked, rising from the table.

"No, sit," her husband said. "I was about to refill mine. So, does anyone's drink need refreshing?

"Holzli's influences could be better," he said as he accepted Mrs. Adler's glass. "He's been chumming around with Eberhard Müller's son."

Mr. Adler prodded pieces to the centers of their squares with a casual finger. When his host left the room, he asked the boy, "Have you ever heard of the Stasi?" He slid a pawn forward.

"No."

"It is the East German secret police. And secret service—it operates both inside and outside the country."

"Like the KGB."

"Yes. The two agencies are associated, of course. In a sense, though, the Stasi has more in common with the Gestapo. It took on all the former Abwehr and Gestapo people it could still find once the heat died down."

Holzli's father came back in. "Pretty much the old outfits with a name change."

"Much the way the United States found positions for Nazi scientific workers," said the Dane.

Holzli saw his father jerk his chin upward and lower it immediately, with no change of expression, as though he had a tic. He knew the man had been stung.

"Well, I don't know that it's quite the same thing," his father said. He set the glasses, down, over carefully. "The people we took on weren't killers, after all."

"Not directly."

"Would you have them go to the Soviets?"

"I do not know that I want anything in particular. I have lost interest in judging how other people should act."

"That may be the hallmark of decadence. Fortunately, decadence is never universal. History always throws up something fresh and vigorous to shoulder the burdens of progress."

Mr. Adler turned his attention back to the game for a few fast exchanges. "Progress," he said, when Holzli slowed things down, hesitating over a capture.

"What?"

"Churchill believed the United States brought about both the Nazi and Soviet regimes by intervening in the first world war. He said that if it had minded its own business, peace would have been made in 1917. I do not see how he can be challenged on that.

"Then, of course, you had to get involved in the next war and hand most of the world over to the Communists. Now, you are fighting them. If you succeed in destroying the Soviets, something else will be let loose—or, more likely, you will have turned yourselves into them."

The snow would not allow the visit to linger on much longer, everyone agreed. It fell without a pause, insistently, blotting out the roads. As the Adlers were leaving, Holzli's father held the chessboard out to them. "You forgot this."

Homework assignments taunted Holzli from the floor at the foot of his bed, where his briefcase had stood since Friday afternoon. He could not have turned to them even if he wanted—the problem with rockets was more urgent. How did they move? He had always assumed that burning fuel pushed them in a simple way, but that illusion had been ripped from before his eyes in the hills last night. He had had a swift, beclouding revelation: Jets had air to push against. Spaceships had nothing.

Where to look for information? He raced through the books in his room that might help, but none of them thought to raise the question. What was upstairs? The encyclopedias might have something.

His parents were reading in the living room. His mother had the collection of Art Buchwald essays he had bought for himself and never yet had a chance to read.

The set of encyclopedias was on the lowest rows of the bookcase. He plopped down and pulled out "PQR." Under "Rockets" was a history and little else. He made a strangling noise.

Across the room, his father set his pipe down and placed his open palm across his pages. "What's the problem?"

"I can't find out how rockets work."

"Why do you need to know that?"

"For school."

"There isn't any mystery to it. Some fuel is ignited and the gas expands out through the back. The rocket is pushed in the opposite direction."

"It pushes against what?"

"It doesn't have to push *against* anything. If there's movement in one direction, there has to be movement in the other direction. It's one of Newton's laws. For every action, there is an equal and opposite reaction. You should be able to find something on that in those." He had taken his pipe up again, and he pointed with the stem toward the bottom shelves.

Holzli pondered this, and it was not sufficient. "But why does that happen?"

His father had gone back to his book. "What? Why does what happen?"

"That something will go in one direction if part of it goes in the other direction. Without pushing against anything."

"What do you mean *why*? There isn't any *why* to it. It's just the way things are." He turned back yet again to his reading with three rapid puffs on the pipe.

The boy took the "MNO" volume with him for appearance' sake; he had no real intention to read it. Uncomfortable as it was, he had his answer. Now, he was more intrigued by the idea that things did not ultimately need reasons. He had never before traced anything back far enough to run up against that wall. It made sense, he guessed, but what followed from it?

At least, he concluded, that some things you just had to live with.

Lunch went quickly, in the garden, eaten while he walked a ring in the snow, trying to kindle heat. He could not have stood to be inside all day, but a few minutes outside were enough to brace him against the hours still to go. The classroom, high above, where the warm air of the entire mansion collected, did not seem so bad.

He put the wrappings and napkin back in the attaché case with the books he had not used so far today and the envelope with the rocket money. The latter could not be left home—he had no good hiding places and there could be no explanation for it less chancy than the inadmissible truth. Then, again, he could not leave the case lying around. He had kept it in arm's reach all day.

That, itself, drew comment. It was, perhaps, a very bad idea, he thought now. It seemed to promote the very interest in the briefcase he least wanted. Smirks followed it about the garden, and unwelcome eyes tracked it up the stairs.

Warming his hands over the radiator, he studied the books and magazines sitting on the windowsill. There were no new books, and he almost ignored the British comics that someone, Mr. Reilly or the Austins, had decided should be available to the students. What path these followed to the school, no one had bothered to ask, as far as Holzli knew. Nearly all were supposed to be weeklies, so most were being routed somewhere else—new issues only showed up every month or two.

If any fresh ones had come in, they would not be here now. Others would have run off with them, to read and pass on to their friends. It would be a fortnight or more before they reappeared on the sill and he had a crack at them.

But, there to the side, was a neat stack of magazines with an unfamiliar *Eagle* on the top. He snatched it up and found the other new arrivals—a *June and School Friend,* and a *Girl,* and a *Lion and Champion.* Everyone read everything, indiscriminately, shamelessly; Kathy at Marvin Grange was as generally popular as Dan Dare.

Delay was too much a luxury. Others could come in at any second. Clutching the comic books, he almost ran toward his desk where he had felt if safe to leave the case out of his reach, this once, in easy sight in an empty room.

The door sprang open with enough force to whack the wall. A torrent of kids roared in. Holzli shoved the magazines under his coat and angled around behind them, too focused on his getaway to see who they were.

He considered going to the library, but it was too public. A back stairway, little used, would have to do. He walked slowly down until he reached the landing between the second and third floors and judged he was safe enough. The cold penetrated there too well for him to take off his coat, but he sat on the floor and pulled out his swag.

When, finally, the bell ran, he started to put the magazines back in his coat but stopped. How would he transfer them to the briefcase without being seen? There was no way to do it. He would have to leave them here and hope to reclaim them after school.

Ten minutes of lunch remained, and half the students had not come back, including Konrad and Mark. Even so, the classroom was a roiled, bubbling mass that would continue to ferment and swell until Mr. Reilly appeared and settled it down. Holzli lifted his case onto his desk and opened it to check on the envelope of money. It was gone.

"Shit!" he screamed.

"Oh, shut up," a girl hissed. He looked up to see that it was Hillary Polt, a crony of Margaret Owens. Her face was congealed disgust, a theatrical mask of revulsion.

"My money's been stolen!" Turning to take in the whole compass of the room, he met bland, controlled innocence on all sides, with, here and there, the suspicion of a smile.

"Just shut up," Hillary repeated. "You're always making an ass of yourself."

All the chemical people concurred by nods or murmurs. All the others turned their eyes away.

He was quiet and intent all through the meal, waiting for his one best opportunity and never sensing it. Between them, his parents never left a breach big enough for him to come in gracefully. In the end, he had to make his opening, breaking in with no transition, distrusting his own treacherous nerve.

"I've got a problem," he intruded into a discussion of eyeglasses and where best to buy them. They hushed, abruptly, surprised and puzzled. At once, before he could fumble the initiative and lose it, he told them all about the rocket project, and the money, and the theft. "It was thirty-two *Franken*. I don't have any way to replace it."

"You should never have taken it from them to begin with," his mother began, but his father waved her silent.

"What's important now is how he handles this. No reason he can't learn something from it. It's perfect, in a way."

To Holzli, he said, "We're not going to give you the money. You're getting older. It's been clear to me for a long time that you need to start developing your social skills. You can't keep bumbling along like you have been, like a child, with no concern for others' responses. You have to learn to take them into consideration, to shape and use them."

He pushed his chair back and pulled the napkin from his collar. "Machiavelli talks about the ways of men and lions and foxes. You need to know all three if you're going to succeed at anything worthwhile. You, though, should start working on the way of the fox."

Glancing to Holzli's mother, he paused, then went on. "We have something to tell you that may help. We didn't want to say anything until we were sure, but it looks like it's go on this. We'll be leaving some time in the first part of next year."

Holzli did not let himself feel anything. He had to be certain what the man was saying. "Leaving Switzerland?" Even asking it betrayed an undignified optimism.

"Yes. We're being transferred to Japan. To Osaka, if you know where that is."

The boy wanted to ask questions, but his father cut them off. "The point is, you won't be here forever. All you have to do is put the Swiss boys off until you're gone. Learn to string them along. Give them reasons why you can't give the money back right away. I could give you the money, but you'll benefit more from this."

There was no point in saying anything. It would only prolong the topic to no purpose. Holzli returned to his food.

"You'll be going to another international school," his mother said. "It was set up by Canadians for missionary kids. It's run by some Reform church, I think."

CHAPTER 28

Mrs. Austin was sitting in her car behind the bus when they boarded it for the athletic hall. Those in the back watched her trail them all the way. Those in the front asked Mr. Reilly what was going on. He answered, without turning from his window, that they would see soon enough.

"Don't bother to change," he told them before letting them get off. "Just go up to our room and stand there, quietly, until we get there." He exited last, and the headmaster's wife waited for him by the door, returning smiles and greetings in kind as the students disembarked.

They played with the equipment and swapped speculation until the door was shouldered open by the teacher carrying a record player. He stood propping the door while Mrs. Austin entered with a stack of LP's on her outstretched arms like a new-baked casserole.

"Move everything to the edges of the room," Mr. Reilly ordered. "Make a big empty area in the middle."

He set up the phonograph on a chair next to the wall, and the albums were placed on another.

At the precise center of the cleared space, he pivoted slowly around to take in the students on every side. "We—or you, rather—are going to learn to waltz. No, don't look like that. It was a dance for soldiers in its day—for warriors and the champions of empire. And their ladies."

Mrs. Austin looked at him and wrinkled her face in a way that conveyed nothing to Holzli. A kind of smile? Loathing? A question? Admiration? Mockery? It was strange enough that the two would work together. Did the Irishman's feelings toward the headmaster extend to the wife? Holzli reminded himself that the feud was all his own hypothesis. Besides, it was not open enough and probably not bitter enough to derail this project and save them all from what was coming.

"So, pair up," the woman said. "Choose partners or we'll choose them for you. Try not to have too much disparity in heights."

She added something so faint that Holzli only heard "this lot." Mr. Reilly laughed.

The two went to the pile of albums and shuffled through them.

"What's this for?" asked Mr. Reilly.

"I want to try something," she said, and they talked in tones too low for Holzli to make out any more.

The students, meantime, did not move except for the gradual coalescence of girls around the permanent pitcher. Holzli observed Mark slipping through the door into the hallway separating the two big rooms on their floor. *Bravo,* he thought, but could not rally the nerve to follow.

Instead, he traced the climbing rope to the ceiling. He had never paid much attention to how it was fastened at the top. It seemed to be suspended from a plate, secured by bolts, with a ring or hook on it. How many bolts there were was not clear; he shifted position and strained to make that out.

"Holzli," he thought he caught in the chatter that filled the air around him.

Glancing about, he saw no one near who might have called his name.

Now that his notice had been drawn to them, it was not clear that the bolts could be strong enough to hold against a person's weight.

"All right, then," Mrs. Austin cried out, slapping her palms together. "Let's start pairing up. You, go with you. And you with you..." Mr. Reilly, too, began matching people up, grabbing shoulders and arms to steer them at each other and fuse them into couples.

"Holzli." The voice was soft and diffident, and, this time, when he turned, a tall, slim, blonde shape had stepped toward him out of the crowd. Vicki White, the object of Mark's fascination and the belle of chemical society.

"Yes?" he managed to say.

"Would you be..." She paused, fixing some problem with the cuff of her sleeve. "Would you be my partner for this?"

It was a trick, he perceived immediately. Vicki was in the inner circle of the Michiganders and would only suggest this to set him up for something. What it was, he could not yet see, but part of the way of the fox, he had read just the night before, was to recognize traps.

"We don't know who we'll be paired up with."

"They just *said* we should choose partners."

"Okay, if you can't get anybody else, I'll be fallback."

Behind her, he saw Mr. Reilly approaching. The teacher pointed to them and said, "Are you two together? Good." The word sealed their union—he moved on before Holzli could gather himself to respond.

The box step was a torment for everyone as they labored to fit their rhythms to the Strauss and each other. To Holzli, whenever he dared split his attention, it looked as though wrestling matches had broken out all through the room.

Other steps, though, once he had them down a little, offered more scope for grace. His body, which had locked into a rigid frame, relaxed and let him feel why the music, till that moment seemingly irrelevant, was being played.

Learning to circle round the room, they ran against another couple, and Holzli apologized before seeing it was Konrad, yoked to Margaret Owens by the adults. Neither was pretending to be happy. The bad energy in that direction drove Vicki and him on past and away.

He wondered where Mark had found to hide. At least he had left before having to watch Holzli dance with Vicki. Who knew what that would have done to him? No one missed him, apparently—an even number of dancers had been left.

"Your friend isn't very good," Vicki murmured near his ear. She had relaxed, too, and softened in his arms. Their bodies came together when he was not careful.

"Who?"

"Müller. He dances like the Tin Man."

It was hard to twirl her when she melted against him. He tried to keep his elbow braced, but his arm tired of that too quickly.

"You boys!" Mrs. Austin shouted over the music. "Take smaller steps! Someday their legs will be shorter than yours! You girls take *very* small steps!"

"Konrad doesn't like Margaret," Holzli said. His voice was hoarse and feeble.

"No one does. But he's always so stiff, anyway. I think all Germans must be like that."

"I don't know many." He bent his arm to relieve the tension on the joint, and she brushed against his pelvis.

Germans bore harder judgments than anyone else, always and everywhere, as far as he could tell. He remembered the Chinese lessons some parents had arranged for their children in Taipei. The arrangement had not lasted long— attendance dwindled over time until everyone gave up on it as an unsalvageable cause.

A young woman, an English major at Taida, had been hired to teach the kids. Bored by the language drills and often unprepared, she improvised lectures on Chinese culture, which most of her pupils preferred, anyway.

Late in the project, when only two German boys and Holzli still showed up, she dropped her introduction of topic constructions to say, without transition, "China and the West are very different. In a German family, if they are eating dinner and there is only one of a thing left, everyone will grab for it. In a Chinese family, everyone will first try to find out if anyone else wants it."

"In most German families," said one of the boys, "I believe everyone will first try to find out if anyone else wants it."

The other boy seconded this.

"No," the girl corrected them, gently. "In a German family, everyone will grab for it."

Vicki's chin rested on his shoulder. "Why do you have a German name? Holzli. Where did that come from? Doesn't it mean a piece of wood or something?"

"It was an uncle's name. He was from Swabia. It's north of here, just across the Rhine. My middle name's 'James'—I've thought of using that instead."

The music stopped, and he let her go. His elbow hurt, and his lower body felt strange. With a shock, he comprehended why that was. He had read about this in whatever sources he could find. That it should happen now—that Vicki should cause it for him while trying to set him up for whatever was planned—was almost funny.

Across the room, the headmaster's wife shook the current Strauss down into his jacket and picked up another record.

"You're putting that on, now?" Mr. Reilly's voice punched through the general din. "Why in the world?"

"Because I like it."

"But it isn't a waltz. A barcarolle isn't even a dance."

"Certainly it is."

"Well, it isn't a waltz,"

"Near enough,"

"The beats are wrong."

"They won't be able to tell the difference. They'll hear the weak beat as a strong. They'll have no difficulties. It's a delightful piece—you should be ashamed for disliking it."

"I don't dislike it. I merely believe it's wrong to confuse the students this early on. Offenbach didn't mean it for a dance—he would have given it a different time signature."

Holzli had had enough. He could not figure out what trick was hanging over his head. Perhaps the joke was simply to experience his awkwardness first-hand and in all completeness, and then laugh about it with the others. He did not care and was not going to wait to find out.

"I'm going to step out for a minute," he told Vicki. "While they're arguing about it."

Mark was not in the hall. He could be anywhere, but the next obvious place was the other room, where the girls met if the classes were not combined.

Under the caged clock on the wall opposite the door, Mark stood holding a basketball between his hands, his shoulders high and tensed. He raised his head and stared when Holzli shut the door behind himself.

"God, you had a good idea getting out of there," Holzli said.

The dark-haired boy bent back to the ball. "This is marvelously made. Is it just a toy?"

"What?" Holzli walked over to see what was distinctive about the ball. "I don't see what you're talking about."

"Watch." Mark threw the thing to the floor with a clumsy, girlish push and caught it on the bounce. "Who crafted this?"

"I don't know. It's a damn basketball. What's wrong with it?"

Mark did not answer. His face glowed with wonder as he turned the ball in his hands. "Everything is so cleanly here, so regular. Like this floor." He ran the sole of his foot over the polished wood.

The eyes came up again and, when they did, Holzli saw something wrong in them. The impression was so sharp he stepped back.

"Do not leave," Mark said. "Please. I must tell you something." His voice, too, was wrong, higher and melodic, lightly lisping. He stooped and laid the ball down, taking care that it not roll.

"What's the matter with you? You're creeping me out."

"You do not know who I am."

Holzli waited, poised to break for the door.

"You think I am Mark, perhaps."

"And..."

"I am not. My name is Regula Schneider. I am not from here."

This was, Holzli knew in a lightening-flash of insight, what had to follow from what went before. Regula had been more and more present for this boy—how else, in the end, could her presence be full and live?

"So, you have taken Mark's body?"

This drew a frown. "This once, with his consent, and never again. But, with his help, I can come through and be here in my own body. As long as he is somewhere I have been."

"I'm going to open the door. I'm not leaving—I just, well, think we should have more air."

He hesitated, fearing an objection, but, getting none, he went slowly to the door and opened the way to the corridor. They had the phonograph going, again, nearly as loud in this room as the other.

"What kind of music is that? It is strange, but it sounds like a dance."

"Do you like it?" He had no plan except to play along.

"I have not danced for so long." Mark was swaying, slightly, in time with the music.

"Why not?"

"We have changed place too often and had to hide too much. And, now, it has been months that I have been a prisoner."

"How a prisoner?"

"We have been run to ground at last. My mother and father are dead already, and soon will come my time."

The face that attended this showed it was no act. Then again, why did the speaker assume so much on Holzli's part?

"They used to drown girls and women. Like my mother. I was trapped just too late, it seems. I will burn like my father. Still, no blood is shed, and that is what concerns them.

"I had not thought to hear a dance again."

He stopped and listened for a space, a smile trembling on his lips.

"They can let blood flow, of course, when they torture. It is only in killing that they limit themselves. Though, even in torture, they have never quite crossed into carnal sin. They are too pious. Everything just short of that transgression."

"You can come through to here, you say. You have a way to escape."

"Yes, if I take it. My resolve changes with each new day. When they let me have a lamp or candle, sometimes I try to hold my finger in the flames. My spirit has not been up to it. I do not know how I could endure the stake.

"And, yet, there is nothing to be won by scarring my finger. I have the world to gain by giving my life. That may be spur enough, finally. There are times, too, when I think on my death with a fierce, bright happiness. More often yet, I am simply at peace with either event, as though the decision were not worth the making, and all will be well whatever I choose.

"Shall I escape?"

"What do you get by dying?"

Mark's smile did not suit a boy. "I get to witness."

"Really, I don't want to have to say. I can't judge and I don't want to."

"My father would have said you are lucky in that. Of course, I can always wait until the final instant and, if I cannot bear the fire, come through then."

Holzli asked himself how far he could cooperate in this without being a fool. His disbelief was no longer whole and sound.

"Mark said your father thought that action leads to the opposite of what you want. Even if you're not being violent."

"Most Baptizers would say my father went too far in many things. But this is just like judgment, and all agree one should not judge lest one be judged. One should not put oneself forward unless one must, my father would have said. It comes back on one.

"That is why Paul writes that it is not his business to judge those outside the church, but only those within. He is free of that burden and its dangers. And all would agree on this."

The connections in this slid through Holzli's grasp. Were there any? Was this at all coherent? Doubt rose in him again like sickness. Mark was quite possibly insane.

"You asked about the price of action. My father always said that evil is divided against itself and works to its own undoing. Good is unitary. There is, at least, no duty to act if one is not moved to it in love and purity of heart."

"Mark also said you wore a married woman's scarf around your hair when you were a child."

"Yes, I did it often, in play. Why do you bring this up?"

"No reason."

It struck Holzli that the music had stopped minutes before. Immediately, the door to the other room shrieked open and released a tempest of shouts and footfalls into the hall.

"Mark has to join the crowd and get back on the bus. Hurry! Let him go!"

As if a plug had been jerked from an outlet, Mark's face dropped all expression. Taking a handful of his shirtfront, Holzli pulled the boy into motion.

The corridor was in enough confusion that they could slip among the bodies undetected. Holzli cast about for Konrad, caught Vicki's eyes instead, and managed to rip his attention away before he read anything there.

Konrad entered the hallway a little before the two grownups. Holzli tried to reach him against the current, but his strength flagged and he was swept from the building. He stayed out of the queue for the bus until Konrad made it down.

"I need to talk to your father."

In the croaks of a reanimated corpse, Konrad said, "I will never experience anything worse than I just have."

"That's fine, but I have to see your father."

"There's no way to do that unless you come home with me. Are you so desperate? Would the telephone do as well?"

"Yes, okay. I only need to be sure of something."

Konrad struggled visibly but overcame his curiosity. "Then, I will meet you downstairs after school. They will let us use the office telephone."

The secretary had left early when they went to use the phone. They knocked on the headmaster's door and were unsure for a few long seconds that he had not done the same, till a thump and muffled clatter let them know there was life within.

Mr. Austin's hair was flattened on the side, and his eyes were bleared. The crease at the corner of his mouth was wet with spittle. "Yes?" he asked, testily.

He had fallen asleep, Holzli realized, but it was still disturbing. A facade had cracked and something showed through that the boy had been satisfied not to see.

Konrad appeared to be unaffected. "Please, sir, if we might use the telephone out here, I need to call my father to pick us up."

"You could have arranged this earlier."

"I know, sir. I was supposed to and forgot."

"All right, I suppose." He waved his arm approximately at the telephone and slouched back behind the door, fumbling it shut.

"Okay," said Konrad. "He should be home all day today."

He dialed and listened, and Holzli looked around the office. The radiator was the same model as upstairs, cast with involved decoration but flaking old beige paint. The building's steam was still on and rattling though the pipes. He held his hand near the iron to gauge its heat.

Too hot for comfort at about three centimeters. Konrad had connected and was explaining the call. When he turned his back, Holzli pressed his palm to the metal ridges and rested his weight on it.

It was impossible. He snatched his hand back and cradled it in the other, bent over and hissing.

"What did you do?" Konrad asked, then told the phone, "Holzli is doing something weird, I do not know what. All right, here he is."

Holzli took the heavy, black receiver with his left hand, not the one with the stinging red stripes. "Hallo, Mr. Müller!"

Working around interruptions, he described the scene in the empty gym.

"There is no dilemma here," said Konrad's father. "Nothing hazy. You have a duty to let his parents know. This is merely an alternative personality Mark has created. It can only 'come through' by supplanting his old one. If that happens, the Mark you know will cease to exist—as, I presume, he wants. But you cannot let it happen. It is a type of suicide."

Holzli made no answer.

"You cannot believe this fantasy is true? Do you?"

"No," the boy mumbled.

"What?"

"No, I don't think it's real."

"Then there is no problem. Tell someone."

"Okay."

"You are positive you do not believe this?"

"Yes."

"Then, goodbye. Tell Konrad not to loiter on his way home."

Hanging up the telephone, Holzli said, "Don't loiter on your way home."

"What about...you know?"

There was a light now under the inner office door. Holzli walked over and knocked.

CHAPTER 29

The earth was bound in ice and shadow. Holzli no longer tried to generate warmth by pacing—he sat sunk in his coat, as like a fetal ball as dignity permitted.

Across the road from the bus stop, someone walked past, then turned and looked at him and crossed.

"Bruno! What are you doing awake?"

"How ya doin'? I must help my aunt with milking. She is ill."

"That is a shame."

"Yes, and it is a shame she is ill."

The American laughed as best he was able. He liked Bruno, but it was too early and too cold for genuine emotion.

"So, Holzli, you are not coming to the *Pfadi* anymore."

"Yes, I am—or I am going to come when I can. When they moved the time up, I could not make the meetings. But my school is just about over for a while, and I will be able to come. And when it gets lighter, and they move the time back, I can always come,"

The fat boy stamped his feet. "What is happening with the rocket? People want to know."

"Oh. Good news. My father has a friend at NASA, an engineer, who has offered to help. He will do it for free, but he is very busy, so he cannot work on it right away. He will get to it before long. I could do it myself, but why not use an expert if we can?"

"That is very nice."

"Yes. As soon as he needs the money for parts, I will mail it to him. Right now, it is hidden in a safe place."

Mark was gone two days after Holzli talked to the headmaster. That was no surprise. Now, however, for the third day running, Konrad had also missed. This was the last week of the term—if he did not return soon, Holzli would not see him for a month.

Mr. Reilly stayed at his desk when they broke for lunch. That removed the best excuse Holzli had for not approaching him. He would never do it at all—never actually *invite* the teacher to talk to him—in any more tractable circumstances.

He stood before the desk, hoping to be noticed so he would not have to take any more of the initiative. His head down, propped by an arm, his fingers spread through his orange hair, Mr. Reilly wrote in a notebook and whispered to himself. There was no help for it; the man was not going to make things easy.

"Sir?" It was almost only an out-breath.

The teacher looked up. "Yes?"

"Could you tell me where Müller has been the past few days?"

The Irishman smiled a broad and nasty smile, and held it for effect. "I'm surprised you don't know. Müller won't be coming back. I understand his family has been expelled from the country. I don't know the details, but I can't say it saddens me.

"Two down, one to go, eh?"

He went back to his writing.

From the kitchen, the radio played song after song to match the season. Sad, now, and complex, music had flirted more with minor keys the more the dark displaced the day. "Eleanor Rigby" suited the near constant night, as did that song by the Left Bank. Anything by Simon and Garfunkel fit the mood.

"The Swiss government made the determination that Mr. Müller was undesirable." His father's smile was subtler than the teacher's, sly, barely a hint.

"Because of his driving?"

"No. Much more to do with his political activities."

"Why would the Swiss care about that? He was anti-American, not anti-Swiss."

"Governments' motives are never quite accountable from the outside. They all have an unknowable inner life. You can never really predict what offers they'll find worth their while.

"Worse things could have happened. You may have done him a greater favor by wandering in front of that car than anyone could ever do intentionally."

Holzli had watched the smile fade. He prodded his vegetables with his fork and listened to the music.

"Son," his father said. "Could you go in and turn that tripe off while we eat?"

CHAPTER 30

The Bahnhof in the town was its own Shop Ville, nowhere near as deeply layered and imposing as Zürich's, but not the clock and ticket-window of his childhood, either. The bus stop, too, was different, an archipelago now of little islands where a fleet of buses docked. Where could they all go from here? In his time, had there even been a second bus?

The main street was closed to traffic and glutted with shops and people. The archway through the gate tower and the cobblestones that ran through it and downhill to the river were their old, grey selves, but the crowd was new—the great swirl of agitated color was never there before. It had been bleakly medieval and now it was a market or a fair.

Away from the city center, he sought the first places he had known. The Cinema Manzo was gone, replaced by a cafe that opened on the street and seemed to connect to the dining room of the hotel. He did not have the heart to enter the hotel itself and inventory changes.

All about was animated, airy and cheerful, alive with people out to enjoy the warmth and sunlight. It was not the town he had carried in his mind three decades and more. Better, perhaps—happier—but not his.

He returned to the bus station by the nearest large street. Here were the cars and trucks denied the town's heart. Behind, and closing, came a car radio hammering him with a bass so loud it hurt. The teenagers inside pulled faces as they cruised past.

Where had the Adlers' apartment been? Not far from here, he thought, but that was the best he could do. He could not pull it up. It did not really matter.

The journey here had started and ended in graffiti, but the country between was as it had been, its surfaces unmarred, its distances pristine. The sun had shone and the land glowed green all the way. That must have happened often in those days, as well, but he did not remember it so.

And people smiled. They had not, then—on that he was sure his memory was true. He had first noticed it in Zürich but made nothing of it, preoccupied with darker changes. There had been laughter, too, amid the other sounds pervading a city once wholly silent.

Industry had grown up in the towns that broke the succession of fields. That was to be expected. The world expanded and filled. Immediately, though, he had known that he had missed an old, forgotten comfort back in the city: the air was clean. It did not hold the smell of cars and chimneys that still seemed cozy to him after all these years. God knew why. Perhaps it had been strongest in winter. He did not associate it with warmth, but, then, he recalled no warm days back then. He admitted them only as abstract necessities.

Even yet, country dominated town. Roads were few and far and empty. Idly, he had watched one flow by at the border of the nearest fields, emerging from the trees that edged it and retreating back again. Suddenly, and too briefly to be certain, he had thought to see an Amish buggy on a clear stretch. The train allowed one meager glimpse and hurried him away.

He found the bus's number on a timetable. It was scheduled to leave almost at once, but he saw no one through its windows, and the driver was standing on its island, looking into the sky.

"*Grüezi,*" he said to the man and was greeted back, and they talked. Having a conversation with someone in a uniform did not suit this place as he remembered it. All talk was cut off, in fact, when they entered the empty bus and it hissed shut on them. They did not speak until the doors opened again.

"*Tschüss*," the driver said as his passenger climbed down into the village.

When the bus came back through, and he reboarded, the driver conceded him recognition, but the return trip was as silent as the first. Only when they reached the town again and had passed out through the doors could anything be said.

He was already walking away when the driver spoke. "I was not sure you knew where you wanted to go. I waited as long as I could before leaving in case you had made a mistake."

How much would the man be willing to hear? In the old days, nothing at all, but, in the old days, he would not have spoken.

"I used to live there, thirty-six years ago."

"That was before my time."

"It was meant to be a lightening raid. In and out before anyone recognized me—if there was any chance of that."

The driver unwrapped a piece of gum with amber fingers and put it in his mouth.

A smoker, trying to quit. Someone who would listen to anything, submit to any distraction.

The bridge had not changed that he could see, nor the river still trying to draw everything to the sea. The schoolhouse had an extension on the front—a police station, the sign said, though the back remained a school. He did not stay to observe more than that.

The neighborhood of his house was so built up that all his private landmarks and signposts were effaced. One of these buildings around him was his, but it wore a disguise, a mask of trimming to cover the concrete face he had last seen. There were no swimming pools; space was at too much of a premium, it appeared, in the clutter of houses and garages and sheds that covered the hill.

He headed up to discover what open ground was left and found the farmers' fields still there on top. The view across the valley must have been much the same, its meadows and woods far prettier than he had ever allowed himself to see. It would often have been out there, available, in this aspect, sunlit, green and tranquil.

Down the valley to his left were two towers that had to be a nuclear plant, its steam an enduring, stationary cumulus casting a moving shadow over the ground. Some part of the valley floor would always be in darkness.

He started back down, hot and sweating in his pullover.

The road over the bridge and past the school divided as it began to ascend the other slope. In the angle of the break was the little grocery his family had used. Dared he go in? So far, he had managed to avoid the locals. He went in.

The woman at the register might have been his age, but who could tell? He mumbled a reply to her greeting, too low to betray his accent. Others were there, shopping, which spread her attention, though a look he thought just short of recognition, a tug of puzzlement, showed every time he glanced her way.

This was not the mix of smells he had expected. It lacked sharpness and character. The cereals were all American brands. He paid for a bottle of water, finally, his lips tight together, ignoring whatever question was in the woman's face.

"But not changed as much as Zürich, I imagine," the driver said. "Of course, you spent the night in the worst place in Zürich, maybe the worst place in Switzerland."

"Why did you say '*Tschüss*' to me?"

"What?"

"No one ever said that when I lived here,"

"You can find the old things if you get away from here. Go to Basel—it's as grey and tired as you could want, and they say '*Adieu*' and '*Merci vielmal*,' and no one has any money."

He had ridden back through the graffiti and was about to leave the train when he realized no one had checked his ticket either way. It was a detail of the past that had escaped him. On all his trips from town to city and back, he had seldom been asked for his pass. And, still, people bought tickets. It was one of the things he had not appreciated, like the lawns he saw through the train window, groomed to military shortness except for the patches where wildflowers were spared.

In the street, he heard a police siren. There had been many of them in the past couple days. As a child, he had only heard that donkey bray once.

He had ceased hoping for much, but there were places he needed to visit for completeness' sake. Crossing the river, he turned south.

The Grebel house had merged with a theater and restaurant. Was the inscription in the wall the same? It read as it had, but he was certain he remembered a separate metal plaque. It was not important—none of his memories, he was learning, counted for a lot, true or false.

The school was represented by a gap in the row of mansions, like the socket of a lost tooth. Some of the others were office space, one a museum. Where the school had been was a garden for the next building over.

The park had been cleared and opened out and reformed into geometrical balance. The elms had been preserved. Wire was wrapped around the one with twin trunks to take up their weight and keep their base from splitting in two. He stood by the biggest, most ancient tree, his old favorite, the one with roots most deeply in the past, and waited until he was satisfied there was nothing to wait for.

Before continuing to Zollikon, he found a bakery and bought a loaf. This, at least, was not a disappointment. Bakers in America never got this right; the inside always turned out dry and hard. They did not understand that the bread should be challenging, not punishing.

The Thomann house was a hotel, remodeled in glass to let the sun in. Vines half hid the courtyard gate, and it would soon disappear behind them altogether. The inscription was there but, again, had it not been a plaque, before? This was his last chance—he waited in the road for anything that might come. He left when a police car came crawling, slow and suspicious, up the hill.

He found a bench and tore off pieces of the bread for birds. They would land and eat however close he put the crumbs. A sparrow lit down right at his foot and stared at him, giving no attention to the bread he dropped in front of it.

"What do you want?" he asked. "This is all I have."

The birds were swept away in a whirlwind of wing and grievance when a car sped by, its windows down, its radio beating the air.

He had hated the old days, anyway, he reminded himself. He was no longer willing to pass judgments. And, he realized, that had never been his responsibility.

He left the plane in Dallas remarkably comfortable, uneasy about his connection but optimistic. Thirty minutes later, he was hot, clammy, ill-tempered and despairing. If there was any air-conditioning, it had been defeated by the heat of the uncountable bodies herded into the holding areas and chutes. All progress had stopped long before.

A tall young woman with hair cropped short and preternaturally red looked in the direction they had once been moving and bent her head to the girl beside her. "They're making us go through security again. Everyone is having to take off their shoes."

"It's nuts," the other said. "We've already been through and we've never left a secure area."

He needed to get his money changed, but that was not going to happen. Sometimes, tiny currents rippled through the mass around him. Usually, it seemed, someone had gotten restless and crowded closer to the person ahead. He inched forward, too, however, and, in the end, was far enough along to join a true flow of movement.

On the other side of the screeners, they were compacted into a hallway and kept there a half hour more. Three empty wooden chairs and a security guard blocked them from the greater part of the hall and its exit doors.

At last, the nearest door opened and a round, middle-aged woman in uniform came out. "Everyone holding an American passport, follow me though this door. The rest of you, go to the door at the end of the corridor and go down the steps."

Their own doorway led to a closed stairwell, and they came out to find the Customs gates. A couple of minutes later, a door at the far end of the room opened, and the foreign passengers emerged.

"Where did they take you?" someone called to the first ones out.

"Nowhere. We just came down the stairs."

The foreigners crossed to the Americans, then were culled out again by signs over the gates.

There was a new element in the air here, an odor beyond sweat and dirt and sour clothes.

The woman who had ushered them down was standing by the ropes. She saw his face and laughed. "All the toilets in this terminal are backed up. It takes a long time to process everyone these days."

At the counter, the officer flipped through his passport. "Welcome home," the man said.

CHAPTER 31

❀

The light died quickly. Night caught the boy at the bridge. There was no moon, and the ceiling of unbroken cloud kept out the stars. The snow that covered everything underfoot and the fog that even now came off the river would have blotted out his remaining sense of place if not for the sound of the water's winter flow. He shuffled to the side until he felt the rail, then followed it across.

From there, he walked by memory. Away from the river, there was no sound at all, and when he rounded the buildings at the bottom of the hill and started up, the quiet was as full as the darkness. The air was black and silent, cold and pure, crystalline. He sensed that it could shatter.

His hands were in his pockets. One was gloved; one wrapped the other glove, which held the little being he had rescued from the ice.

A bend and a rise, and he was among houses with windows that gave him yellow light. Another rise, and his own house was glowing above. He had a goal, now, a haven to aim for, a store of warmth and illumination.

Ice crusted on the wool around his nose and mouth where his breath froze. It sawed against his lips. He could only trust his feet were all right—they had no feeling, but they seemed to be carrying him. He lowered his head and pushed on.

Reaching home, he rushed to thaw his hands in the sink; they were close to useless, and he had almost been trapped outside the house, unable to open the door. He was careful to twist each knob through precisely the same angle. It was a safeguard; he could not judge the water's temperature.

Everything began to sting—his hands, his toes, his ears. He undressed, then encased himself in flannel. He was gathering his wet things to carry to the laundry room when he remembered the animal in his coat.

Cupped in his hand, it was smaller than he had thought. He could not see it breathe. Holding it in hot water did nothing. He took his good shoes out of their box and lined it with socks. Folding a handkerchief about the creature, he put it in and set the box under his desk lamp.

He checked on it from time to time in the next few days, but it never moved and he finally gave it up for dead.

www.ingramcontent.com/pod-product-compliance
Lightning Source LLC
Chambersburg PA
CBHW060806120626
46557CB00001B/105